MURDER, MARIGOLDS & MEZCAL

A DIA DE LOS MUERTOS COZY CULINARY MYSTERY

GRETA SINCLAIR

❀ Formatted with Vellum

INTRODUCTION

Food critic and amateur sleuth Darcy Finnegan expected Oaxaca to be a feast of mole, mezcal, and marigolds—not murder.

But when **a notorious American art dealer is found impaled on a towering sculpture** during the Day of the Dead festival, Darcy, her bestie, and **loyal Schnoodle Mozart,** are pulled into a mystery as vivid and layered as the city itself.

The victim had enemies on every continent, but it's his exploitation of local artisans that has tempers flaring and suspects emerging—from a betrayed woodcarver and a scorned lover to a rival exporter with a grudge.

Things grow even more complicated when Interpol agent Marcus Evans, Darcy's **unpredictable former flame,** shows up undercover.

With one sculpture missing and danger lurking behind every painted face, Darcy must navigate a maze of lies and loyalties.

In a city where tradition and treachery intertwine, **can**

Darcy uncover the truth before the killer vanishes into the night?

☆☆☆☆ " Another great read in this series.This time Darcy, Lizzie, and Mozzie are caught in a murder investigation in Oaxaca, Mexico, during the Dia de los Muertos festivities. The descriptions of the Mexican traditions are first-rate, and the mystery is gripping right to the end since there are many suspects. —Ingrid S. (Austria)

☆☆☆☆☆"Another great story—a favorite of the series!"

—A.E. Pollison

☆☆☆☆☆"Riveting: Unputdownable. Did not see the end coming!" — Rotty3M

☆☆☆☆☆"I LOVE this book! If I could give it six stars, I would! A perfect addition to the series!" — C. Poteet

MURDER, MARIGOLDS & MEZCAL

by

Greta Sinclair

CANDLES, CARVINGS, AND A CORPSE

In Oaxaca, they light candles to honor the dead—someone lit theirs early this year.

I stepped off the plane into a wall of late October heat, thick with the scent of burning copal wood and simmering spices. Mozart sneezed the second we hit the open air and promptly tried to lick a marigold off the arrivals mural. Lizzie, naturally, was already ten paces ahead, dragging her roller bag like it carried dead weight. I grimaced.

Please, just once... nothing dead on this trip.

"Smell that, Darcy Finnegan?" she said, spinning on her heel in the middle of the pedestrian lane. "Cinnamon. Smoke. A hint of accidental tequila."

"And that's just your suitcase," I muttered, hoisting Mozart into the crook of my arm before he could decorate the customs banner with something unspeakable.

Oaxaca in late October is a city draped in memory and marigolds. The streets breathe with music, the walls bloom with paper flowers and murals of skeleton brides, and the scent of mole wafts through the cracks in centuries-old stone. It's as if the entire city paused to welcome the dead with a parade, a prayer, and a potluck. And, as an international food critic, I was here to soak it all in and write about it. Lizzie, my photojournalist pal, was here to take pictures.

We were still blinking against the sensory overload when a man in a rumpled linen shirt barreled past us, phone in one hand and ego in the other. He zeroed in on the last available taxi like a heat-seeking missile. Unfortunately, someone else was already opening the door.

She was youngish—I'd say in her thirties—with a traveler's tan and the kind of calm that made Mozart stare. She clutched a paper-wrapped bundle in both arms, like it might bite if she dropped it. I was just turning to comment when Rumpled Linen Man bumped into her, snatched the cab door and package out of her hand, barked something in English about a "tight schedule," and wedged himself inside before she could protest.

Lizzie gasped. "Darcy, did he just—he did. Oh, he *so* did."

The woman didn't yell. She didn't argue. She just stood there, expression unreadable, hands clenched. And in that moment, as the cab sped off with its smug new occupant, she looked like someone holding back an entire landslide.

Mozart growled low in my arms.

"Rude," Lizzie quipped. "Not Mozart. Him."

I agreed with both.

We watched the cab disappear into traffic like a thief in the night. The woman he'd left behind didn't move. Didn't curse. Just stared after it like she'd seen a ghost slip into the backseat and slam the door behind it.

Lizzie leaned toward me. "Well, that was a flaming pile of festive. Should we offer her our ride? Or do we just let chivalry die here at the curb with that poor girl's dignity?"

"I vote we offer."

Our driver, a sleepy-eyed man with a decal of Frida Kahlo

on his dashboard and a half-eaten tamale on the console, was in no rush. I turned toward the young woman, now visibly pale beneath her sun-worn skin.

"*¿Necesitas ayuda?*" I asked gently. "We've got space, if you want to ride with us."

She looked up—startled, I think. There was a flicker of something I couldn't name in her eyes. Not just a surprise. Something sharper. Fear?

She opened her mouth. Closed it. Then her eyes darted to the ground, scanning like she'd dropped something.

"My package," she said.

Mozart let out a little whuff, ears pricking.

She turned in a slow circle, hands fluttering at her sides. "It was wrapped. Long. Brown paper. I—I had it right here—"

"I think maybe he took it. When he shoved past you?"

Her breath hitched. She looked toward the road, but the taxi was long gone.

Lizzie stepped in. "You want us to follow him and dramatically throw ourselves on the hood? I've had worse ideas."

I shot her a look. "Come with us," I offered again. "It's a short ride. We'll help however we can."

The young woman hesitated, eyes flitting from me to the dog in my arms. Mozart gave her his best soulful stare, the one that made airline employees give him extra peanuts.

She nodded. "Thank you," she said. "My name is... María."

María. Simple. Unassuming. And, if I was any judge of people—and I was—completely fake. I smiled anyway and opened the door. The moment she slid in, she wrapped her arms tightly around herself, and the silence that followed was too loud to ignore.

As we pulled into traffic, the city unfurled around us in marigold-colored motion. Food carts smoked on corners. Children carried papier-mâché skeletons in backpacks. The streets pulsed with the living and shimmered with the memory of the dead.

Beside me, María didn't blink. I made a note to keep an eye on her. And in my mind, I wrote the first line of what I was certain would be a very complicated recipe.

One stolen taxi. One shaken stranger. And a pinch of something no one wanted to say out loud.

Mozart licked my hand once, as if to confirm it.

We weren't even at the hotel yet, and I already knew—

Someone in this city was lying through their teeth.

* * *

OFFERING WAS PURE KISMET. As it turned out María was staying at the exact same hotel as we were. The cab dropped us on a cobbled side street framed by bursts of bougainvillea and the sharp scent of lime and exhaust.

Casa de las Bugambilias, or House of the Bougainvilleas, was tucked behind a painted gate with a mosaic of a hummingbird mid-flight, like it had paused just long enough to welcome us before vanishing again. Inside, the world shifted—no longer the bustle of the *mercado* or the pulse of the parade, but a courtyard haven that felt more like staying with your favorite aunt who collected art, cooked like a saint, and had an eye for color that made your soul exhale.

The hotel wasn't posh in the polished-marble, hushed-lobby sense. It was homey, vibrant, and utterly Oaxacan. Bright textiles spilled over tiled benches. Bougainvillea vines draped the archways like they'd chosen fashion over function. Each room had its own personality—some with hand-carved headboards, others with hand-painted sinks shaped like calla lilies, and all of them infused with a kind of curated warmth that didn't need to try too hard. The air smelled faintly of orange blossom, candle wax, and something else—maybe cinnamon, maybe memory.

At the heart of it all was the dining patio, where mismatched chairs surrounded a long, colorful table under *papel picado,* cut paper flags that danced in the breeze. It was the kind of place where breakfast wasn't a service, it was a ritual. The kind of place that wrapped around you slowly, until you forgot to check your phone or your return ticket.

It didn't feel like a hotel. It felt like someone had turned their love for Oaxaca into a home—and invited you to stay.

Our driver popped the trunk with a grunt and gestured lazily toward the tiled path.

"I love it," Lizzie said. "It smells like citrus and secrets."

I glanced back at María, who stood perfectly still as if bracing for something—recognition, maybe, or judgment. Neither came. Lizzie was too busy cooing at the terra cotta planters shaped like skulls and Mozart had found a lizard to obsess over.

Inside, we were greeted by a woman with a clipboard and an expression like she could sniff out unauthorized guests by scent alone. María offered a polite thank you and disappeared into the hallway after murmuring something about meeting a friend. No luggage. No room key. Just vanished.

Lizzie raised an eyebrow. "Well, she's mysterious."

"And then some."

Something nibbled at my brain that made me wonder—was she really a guest here?

I didn't have a chance to linger on it long. We barely had time to drop our bags before Lizzie dragged me out again, insisting we couldn't waste "prime festival hours" on unpacking. Within minutes, we were swept up in the pulse of the city—*alebrijes* towering in shopfronts, *papel picado* fluttering like prayers overhead, and every corner humming with drums, laughter, and the smell of anise and fire-roasted corn. It was intoxicating.

Until we turned a corner and found ourselves face-to-face with the *mercado*. That's where everything changed.

The *Mercado de Artesanías*, the Artisan Market, hit me like a fistful of confetti and a *marimba* solo to the solar plexus.

Color exploded in every direction—walls draped with woven shawls in shades of paprika and sapphire, flower stalls bursting with golden *cempasúchil* blooms—the fluffy blooms of Mexican marigolds—and tables piled high with sugar skulls smiling like they knew secrets they weren't telling. The air smelled like roasted chilies, beeswax candles, cinnamon, and just the barest hint of impending financial regret.

Mozart sneezed violently for the fourth time and looked up at me with watery eyes, thoroughly betrayed.

"I told you not to sniff the *mole* powder," I muttered, fishing a tissue from my pocket as he snuffled again. "You have no one to blame but yourself."

Lizzie, meanwhile, was already halfway to a stall selling miniature coffins filled with tiny chocolate skeletons.

"Are these edible or just emotionally symbolic?" she asked the vendor cheerfully, already pulling out her pesos.

"Both," I said, tugging her back gently by the elbow. "Come on."

The crowd surged around us—locals chatting animatedly, tourists overwhelmed by beauty and bargaining, children darting between stalls in face paint and butterfly wings. The *mercado* was alive in the way cities rarely are anymore—messy and loud and entirely uninterested in catering to expectations.

We passed a towering sculpture near the central fountain, and Lizzie stopped short.

"Okay, what in the name of Guillermo del Toro is *that*?"

I followed her gaze. The creature was at least ten feet tall, a jaguar with spiraling eyes, fanged jaws, and wings that looked suspiciously like they could flap. Dangerous claws tipped its paws. Its painted pelt shimmered in red and deep indigo, the patterns so intricate they seemed to move if you stared too long. It was mounted on a carved base, like some ancient guardian with opinions about your footwear.

"That," I said, "is an *alebrije.*"

Lizzie gave me the side-eye. "I'm sorry, what-now?"

"*Alebrije.* A traditional folk art sculpture—part spirit guide, part fever dream, all cultural icon. They're usually made of papier-mâché or carved wood and painted in colors that make Crayola look shy. Originated in Mexico City, but the woodcarving ones like this are a specialty of Oaxaca."

Lizzie tilted her head. "So...spirit animals that moonlight as art pieces?"

"Basically. They protect you, guide you, and occasionally star in your nightmares."

"Love that for us."

Mozart barked softly at the base of the sculpture, then immediately sat down like he'd finished his civic duty and could now expect a treat.

"See?" I said, handing him a biscuit from my pocket. "Mozart gets it."

We wandered deeper into the chaos. Every few feet, I caught snippets of hushed conversations—vendors whispering behind their hands, glancing toward one another with the kind of furtive concern that didn't pair well with tourism or open-air commerce.

A sudden shift in the atmosphere drew my attention.

He entered like a man who assumed the air rearranged itself just for him.

Tall, tanned, and smug enough to have his own zip code, he wove through the crowd with a camera in one hand and the kind of practiced grin that came with very expensive dental work. His shirt was rumpled linen—white, naturally, because nothing says "I summer in Capri" like a wardrobe incapable of hiding dirt—and his sunglasses were the kind that doubled as a mirror, which meant I had the pleasure of watching myself scowl at him in real time.

He paused to photograph the winged jaguar *alebrije*—first from a distance, then up close, zooming in on the fangs like he was documenting a trophy kill. Then he pivoted to take a selfie with it, angling for the best lighting like the creature was just a backdrop in the epic saga of his own reflection.

"Who's Captain Charm?" Lizzie asked, slipping beside me and adjusting her oversized sunglasses.

"No idea," I said, "but if his ego gets any bigger, it's going to require its own altar."

Mozart let out a low growl, soft but unmistakable. I bent down and scratched behind his ears.

"I know, bud," I whispered. "I don't like him either."

We watched as Rumpled Linen strutted deeper into the *mercado,* oblivious to the looks he was getting—not awed or admiring, but sharp-edged, wary.

We hadn't made it ten feet past the feathered *lucha libre* wrestling masks when a sharp voice sliced through the hum of the mercado.

"*¡Estas no son souvenirs!*" These are not souvenirs.

I turned in time to see a young woman—late twenties maybe, all angles and intensity—snatch an *alebrije* out of Rumpled Linen's hands with the same energy I reserve for snatching Mozart away from anything that smells like sardines.

"Oh, come now, Catalina, I thought we were practically family," he muttered, looking more wounded than apologetic. "You know… *mi casa, su casa?*"

"It's *not* for sale," the woman snapped, switching to

English with barely veiled disgust. Her accent curled around the words like a blade.

I watched as she clutched the *alebrije* to her chest—like a shield, or maybe a lifeline—and turned her back to the man without another word. Her shoulders were stiff, chin tilted high. Even from where I stood, however, I could see her fingers tremble slightly as she adjusted the detachable tail. Rumpled Linen laughed coldly, shrugged, and moved away.

"Someone skipped their *mezcal* this morning," Lizzie said beside me, sipping water from a plastic bottle. "That was some serious don't-touch-my-stuff energy."

"She wasn't wrong," I murmured, eyes still on the woman.

She exhaled slowly, like she was trying to release something heavy. Then her posture shifted. Her hand shot to her mouth. Her eyes fluttered shut, jaw clenched. For a moment, I thought she was going to scream.

Instead, she gagged. Just once. Then she spun on her heel and vanished around the corner of the booth, shoulders hunched like she'd been gut-punched by something no one else could see.

Mozart barked once—sharp, alert—and trotted a few steps in her direction before looking back at me.

"She okay?" Lizzie asked, crinkling her brow.

"I don't know," I said. "I feel like something's off."

Mozart sat, ears forward, gaze fixed on the empty space where the woman had disappeared.

"Is she sick?" Lizzie offered. "Food poisoning? Nerves? Sudden realization that toe rings are back in fashion?"

I raised an eyebrow. "Your compassion is staggering."

Lizzie shrugged and shook her water bottle. "No worries here."

I gave her a playful punch in the shoulder. "You're a menace."

"I prefer, prepared."

Mozart let out a little huff, like he agreed with both of us, then resumed his post beside my ankle. He kept looking toward that corner, though.

I glanced that way again too. Whoever she was, she hadn't just snapped at a tourist. She'd cracked—just for a second—and whatever slipped through the fissure had left a mark. I didn't know who she was. Didn't stop me from harboring a feeling we hadn't seen the last of her.

And my gut, which had a frustratingly good track record with these things, whispered she wasn't just any artisan. She was a question mark—and someone, somewhere in this *mercado*, was already scribbling answers in the margins.

We were looping back toward the plaza fountain—Lizzie on the hunt for something "festive but fierce" to wear to tomorrow's vigil, Mozart in hot pursuit of a roasted corn husk—when I caught sight of a familiar linen-shirted menace.

He wasn't selling anything. Of course, he wasn't. He didn't look like the type who got his hands dirty with inventory. No, he was circling a vendor's dragon carvings like a big-game hunter too lazy to load his own rifle. Camera in one hand, he was crouching, zooming, clicking—cataloging every inch of the display with the hungry precision of someone who didn't care what the art meant, only what it could make him.

"These patterns?" he said, mostly to himself but loud enough for the tourists nearby to hear. "Incredible. Pre-colonial influence with contemporary pop. God, the marketing writes itself."

The vendor looked annoyed but said nothing. Maybe he didn't understand the words—or maybe he understood them too well and was choosing silence over blood pressure.

I stopped just beside a display of painted hummingbirds, watching him angle for the perfect shot. His camera beeped as he captured the swirling tail of a cat sculpture in striking red and indigo.

"Unique," he muttered. "Mass appeal. Limited run. Not *too* limited, though."

Before I could make another mental snark about copyright infringement and moral bankruptcy, someone else stepped in.

"That piece was never yours, Vale."

Linen Shirt—Vale, apparently—straightened slowly, the corner of his mouth already curving into a smug half-smile. "Possession is nine-tenths of art dealing, Molina."

Ah. Two names. A whole tangled string of implications.

The man now standing across from Vale—Molina—looked like he'd walked out of a cigar lounge where the real deals happened in whispers and handshake bribes. Late thirties, crisp shirt, leather belt with just enough edge. He didn't posture. He didn't blink. He just looked at Vale like he was something tracked in on the bottom of a custom boot.

"You're sloppy," Molina said. "You don't ask permission, don't grease the right palms. You show up, flash a camera, and act like the whole city owes you inspiration on a platter."

"I don't need permission, Gerardo," Vale replied, flashing teeth. "Inspiration's public domain."

Molina's fingers twitched—like they were used to signing checks and occasionally throwing punches. "You keep treating sacred art like trend bait and the wrong person's going to make an example of you."

"Right," Vale said, stepping in closer, just enough to make Mozart bristle. "Because *you* have so much respect for the craft."

"I have respect for the rules."

It wasn't about honor. It was about territory.

Mozart growled—a low, vibrating warning that made Vale glance down briefly.

"Easy, Mozart," I said, running a hand along his back. "No need to defend the morally ambiguous."

Lizzie leaned in, licking mango from her thumb and snapping a picture with the other hand. "Oooh. This is like Shark Tank, except everyone's a little bit more murder-y."

Vale didn't bother to respond. He gave Molina one last tight smile and melted back into the crowd, camera bouncing off his chest.

Molina stayed behind, watching him vanish, jaw clenched just enough to betray how badly he wanted to follow.

Mozart kept staring at Molina, ears up. Not wagging. Just watching.

I was watching too. Not because I knew who these men were. Instead, I was relying on the one thing I'd learned traveling the world with a dog and a deadline. The louder the charm, the bigger the mess behind it.

And something about these two told me the mess was only just beginning.

We hadn't gone far when Mozart trotted left instead of right, dragging me past a pyramid of hand-embroidered blouses and straight toward a small booth tucked between two juice carts. It was quieter here—less tourist traffic, more purposeful pacing—and the first thing I noticed was the display: a professionally printed banner in bold magenta with white text that read:

PROTECTING CULTURAL HERITAGE | Preserving Indigenous Art, One Carving at a Time.

The second thing I noticed was the woman manning it.

Mid-forties, pressed white blouse with the sleeves rolled, elegant but no-nonsense glasses, and an expression that could probably curdle milk. She stood beside a glass case displaying confiscated forgeries, each tagged and labeled like museum specimens.

And she was staring daggers at Vale.

I recognized her name from the plastic badge clipped neatly to her belt: **Dr. Soledad Pineda**, with smaller text below it that read *UNESCO Affiliate / Oaxaca Chapter Director.*

Lizzie leaned closer to squint. "What's she a doctor *of* ? Museum Justice?"

"Art history and international law, if I had to guess," I murmured, stepping just close enough to eavesdrop without drawing fire.

Vale was flipping through a rack of artisan postcards on a spinning display like he was killing time before his next offense. He barely looked up before she struck.

"Selling sacred art without provenance makes you a thief, not a dealer," she said, voice clipped and cool as a marble slab.

Vale turned, visibly unimpressed. "I'm not selling anything. Just appreciating."

Dr. Pineda's smile didn't feel genuine. "You appreciate it by asking questions. Not by snapping pictures and calling it marketable."

He chuckled, all easy arrogance. "Relax, Doc. I'm not the villain in a documentary."

That flicker.

Just a glint of something in his eyes—uncertainty. Nerves, quickly masked with charm. I wasn't fast enough to fool someone who watches men flinch for a living. Or dogs.

Mozart took a step forward and sat like a sphinx, staring up at Dr. Pineda like he'd found a kindred spirit.

"Funny," Vale said, turning back to the postcard rack. "You cultural watchdogs bark louder every year."

"No," Dr. Pineda replied. "We just bite more efficiently."

Before I could duck behind the sugar skull stand to write that line down, Lizzie spoke.

"I mean… she's not wrong. Still, that typeface is *heinous.* Should I offer to help with their brochure?"

"Don't even think about it," I hissed, grabbing her elbow and steering her away before she could start pitching a redesign involving biodegradable ink and iconography that "honors tradition while embracing modernity."

As we retreated, I glanced over my shoulder.

The doctor hadn't moved. Still standing guard, arms crossed, unmoved by Vale's smug indifference.

He had no idea how outmatched he was.

And Mozart did too—he let out one last huff of agreement as we melted back into the crowd.

"You know," Lizzie said as we passed a stall selling miniature *alebrijes* carved from avocado pits, "if I ever get into trouble, *that's* the woman I want in my corner."

I nodded. "Fair. But also? That's the woman I don't want *anyone* to cross."

Because if Vale had made a habit of poking cultural lions with a copyright stick, he'd just poked the wrong one.

And something told me Dr. Soledad Pineda didn't just keep receipts. She filed charges.

Twilight in Oaxaca crept in like a whispered secret—soft at first, then sudden, as if the city had blinked and swapped its palette. The bright buzz of midday melted into deep orange shadows, the kind that stretched across stone and turned papel picado into lace silhouettes.

Festival lights clicked on one by one overhead, casting a warm, shimmering glow over the plaza. Strings of marigold garlands danced in the rising breeze, and somewhere nearby, a flute struck a haunting tune that made Mozart pause mid-sniff.

"Is it just me," Lizzie said, tucking a strand of hair behind her ear, "or did the market go from 'Disneyland of the Dead' to 'emotionally charged ghost story' real fast?"

"It's not just you," I murmured.

Because something *had* shifted.

The chatter was still there—vendors bargaining, kids laughing, musicians tuning up. Underneath, something else pulsed. Not quite silent. Not quite dreadful. A hum. Subtle, electric. Like the whole place was holding its breath.

Mozart let out a quiet whuff and angled his body toward the far side of the square. And that's when I saw her. Across the plaza, framed by the rising glow of hanging lanterns, stood María. Or whatever her name really was.

She hadn't seen me. Or if she had, she wasn't reacting. She stood completely still—unnaturally still—arms at her sides, chin slightly dipped, eyes locked on something ahead of her.

I followed her gaze.

Vale.

He was holding court near the giant winged jaguar *alebrije* in the square, laughing too loudly at something no one else seemed to find funny. A thin ribbon of smoke curled up from a grill behind him, mingling with the faint haze of incense that drifted from the altar stalls nearby. In one hand he held a small glass of *mezcal,* which he raised dramatically toward the crowd like he was toasting his own brilliance as he took selfies with the winged jaguar.

María didn't move. Didn't blink. Just stared at him like she was trying to memorize the shape of him. Or erase it.

I took a step forward. Then another. Before I could call out—before I could even lift a hand—she was gone. One blink and she'd vanished, swallowed by the shifting tide of festival goers, paper lanterns, and carved shadows.

"Did you see—" I started.

"Who?" Lizzie asked, holding a sugar skull in one palm.

"No one," I said, scanning the crowd again. "Just… no one."

Mozart pulled. Not hard—just a gentle, persistent tug on the leash, like he'd caught a scent not of food. No, it was feeling. I followed his lead past a row of carved skulls stacked like they were waiting for a game of artisan Jenga, then through a thin crowd near the edge of the *mercado* where the noise thinned and the color faded.

He stopped in front of a pair of wooden doors. Old, splintered, sun-faded.

A withered wreath of marigolds—dried out but still golden—hung crookedly from the left door. Below it, a single white candle flickered in the shadow of a ceramic holder shaped like a jaguar's head. It wasn't one of the mass-produced ones I'd seen in the stalls. This one was old. Handmade. Its teeth were chipped, and the glaze had spidered with time.

There was no merchandise on display. No signage with prices. Just a tarnished metal plaque bolted above the lintel that read:

Taller de Don Abel Flores.

Workshop of Don Abel Flores.

Mozart sat, then let out a soft whine—not distressed, not excited. Just... reverent.

Lizzie appeared beside me, mango *paleta*, or popsicle, now long gone, expression suddenly sobered. "Looks like a shrine."

She wasn't wrong. I shook my head.

"No," I murmured. "A shrine celebrates someone. This feels more like an apology."

The marigolds weren't arranged with care—they'd been placed, almost guiltily, like someone couldn't leave without leaving something. The candle wasn't part of a display—it was a vigil. Silent. Half-forgotten. Still... burning.

There were faint burn marks at the base of the door. A

scar. Old smoke damage, maybe. The kind that remained long after the flames were gone.

Lizzie reached for the doorframe like she wanted to knock, then thought better of it and tucked her hand into her bag instead. "Who's Don Abel?"

"I don't know."

My pulse had quickened in that irritating way it always did when a breadcrumb fell into my path. Mozart pressed close to the threshold, nose twitching once… then twice… then, as if satisfied, he turned and sat again. Guarding.

I crouched beside him and whispered, "You found something, didn't you?"

His ears pointed forward. In Mozart-speak, that was a definitive yes.

Lizzie exhaled beside me. "I was hoping for a fun, murder-less vacation."

I gave her a sideways glance. "You brought me."

"Okay, but can we not have at least one market without a looming sense of ancestral guilt?"

"Probably not," I said, standing. "Look on the bright side."

"There's a bright side?"

I gestured to the flickering candle and the jaguar-shaped holder. "At least no one's dead."

That's when we heard the scream.

GOSSIP AND GHOSTS

The scream sliced through the night like a hot knife through *queso de hebra*, string cheese.

For half a second, I thought it was part of the music—some dramatic flourish from a brass band in the next square over. Then Mozart's ears pricked, and he bolted.

"Wait—Mozart!" I stumbled after him, Lizzie close on my heels, still clutching her half-eaten *churro* like it might serve as a defensive weapon.

We followed the noise to the central plaza, where a cluster of people had gathered beneath the towering winged jaguar *alebrije*—the same one that had caught our eye earlier. The lights around the market flickered and danced, casting long shadows across the sculpture's painted face.

Mozart came to a sudden stop, planted his paws, and barked once—sharp, alert, almost reverent.

And that's when I saw him.

Rumpled Linen. Vale was slumped forward, draped awkwardly against the base of the carving. One arm dangled loose, the other twisted oddly at his side, and his head lolled at an unnatural angle. His rumpled linen shirt was darkened in places, and the winged jaguar's carved front claw, the one that jutted out from its paw like a weaponized flourish, had plunged directly between his shoulder blades.

Even in the half-light, it was clear: he wasn't napping.

"Holy *mole*," Lizzie breathed beside me.

Mozart whimpered and backed up a step, pressing against my calf.

"How does something like that happen?" Lizzie added, still staring as if her brain hadn't quite caught up with her mouth.

Behind us, someone murmured in Spanish—an older woman with a lace shawl wrapped tightly around her shoulders. *"Es la maldición."*

"The curse," I translated automatically, mostly for Lizzie's benefit.

That did the trick.

She paled a shade. "You don't think...?"

"I think," I said carefully, "that you don't wind up looking like an Oaxacan *paleta* by accident."

She made a soft, strangled sound. "A popsicle? Could we not use food metaphors right now?"

Fair enough.

The crowd had started to grow, everyone doing that awkward half-circle thing where they wanted to see but not be seen looking. Whispers rippled—some in English, most in Spanish—none of them helpful.

Someone said he was drunk. Someone else said he slipped. Another blamed the wind, which struck me as optimistic. I wasn't listening to the speculation. I was cataloguing.

The claw had gone in between his shoulder blades, deep—not high. He would've had to be *right there* for it to hit—either a fall or, more likely, a push.

There were no overturned crates nearby. No broken

decorative fencing. Just glimmering lights, stunned faces, and one towering guardian with blood on its claws. Mozart let out another quiet whine and pressed against my ankle again. I reached down and smoothed a hand along his back, more for me than him.

"He was posing next to it earlier," I murmured. "Taking selfies. He was—alive."

Lizzie looked at me, eyes wide. "Do you think he got drunk and tried to climb it for a better angle?"

"Maybe," I said, though I didn't believe it. "Or maybe someone made sure his last photo was picture-perfect."

The first whistle cut through the murmuring crowd like a slap, sharp and commanding. Then came the shouts. Two officers in crisp navy uniforms pushed their way through the onlookers, radios crackling in a mix of Spanish and static. One of them immediately began ushering people back with firm, controlled gestures, repeating, *"Por favor, retrocedan. Mantengan la distancia."*

Please back up. Maintain your distance.

Behind them, a small white police truck pulled to the curb. Its lights spun red and blue against the colorful paper banners strung overhead, turning the plaza into a surreal mix of celebration and crime scene.

A third officer emerged, older than the others and with a practiced calm that suggested he'd seen worse. His badge read **Gómez**. He approached the base of the *alebrije,* squinted once at the body, and muttered something under his breath I didn't quite catch.

Lizzie leaned in. "Did he just say what I think he said?"

"I think he called it a *trágico accidente,"* I murmured. "A tragic accident."

She snorted. "That doesn't look like falling. That looks like posing."

She wasn't wrong.

Another officer had retrieved a folded gray blanket from the back of the truck and now carefully stepped around the carving's base to cover the body. I caught one last look at the way the man's neck twisted—too cleanly. No bruising on his arms. No scrapes on his palms. Nothing that said he'd tried to catch himself or break a fall. No panic. No struggle. Just... placement.

Mozart gave a soft growl beside me, not threatening—just wary.

Officer Gómez conferred with his team briefly, then pulled a small notebook from his back pocket. He gestured for a few of the surrounding vendors to step forward. One woman—her apron still dusted with flour—nodded solemnly and began describing what she'd seen, which, judging from the pantomime, hadn't been much.

Lizzie elbowed me. "Do we stay?"

I shook my head. "We observe. Discreetly. We're tourists."

"Right. Tourists with a front-row seat to murder."

I glanced down at Mozart, who had finally stopped growling. He stayed glued to my side, nose twitching as if filing everything away for later.

Officer Gómez looked up then, scanning the crowd like he could feel something still wasn't right. His eyes passed over me and moved on without pause.

Good.

We were just faces in the crowd. For now. I'd seen enough crime scenes, though, to know that sometimes, the best clues weren't left behind. They were standing three feet away, wrapped in a blanket, scribbling notes in the dark, or slinking off before the questions started. And one of those people had just made sure Curtis Vale would never take another selfie.

The officers began stringing yellow tape across the edges of the plaza, cordoning off the winged jaguar carving like it might leap up and attack someone else. The crowd, now swelling with the kind of hushed urgency that only tragedy can summon, pressed back reluctantly.

I took a step farther out of the way. Not retreating, exactly. Instead, my eyes scanned the gathering faces, looking not for guilt, necessarily. No, I was looking for recognition. Shock. Absence. Something.

Near the edge of the market stalls stood the young woman we'd seen have words with Vale and then get sick. Catalina. The sharp, protective energy she'd wielded earlier was gone now, replaced with something brittle. Her arms hung stiff at her sides. Her face was pale, and her mouth worked silently like she couldn't quite find the breath to speak.

Beside her stood an older man. Broad-shouldered, lined face, hands like they'd held knives or carving tools for decades. His arm was around her, holding her just close enough to be protective without smothering. His jaw was clenched, his eyes fixed on the body the way one might study a fault in a finished piece—tight, grim, unspeaking.

He looked like someone who'd seen death before and still hated the sight of it. Something about him—his posture, his gravity—made me feel like I should know who he was.

Not far off, I spotted the man from earlier—the one with the slick shirt and even slicker expression. The one Vale had called Gerardo Molina. He stood with his arms crossed, mouth set in a hard line, eyes narrowed in deep, calculating thought. Not grief. Not horror. Strategy.

He wasn't surprised. I'd seen that look before. In boardrooms. In back alleys. It was the face of a man mentally adjusting to a new opportunity.

Just beyond him, I caught sight of the woman from the NGO booth—the one with the piercing stare and the UNESCO badge. Dr. Pineda. She was speaking quietly to a young officer, her voice low, her expression unreadable. Not cold. Controlled. Intentionally blank.

She gestured once toward the sculpture, then paused and glanced toward the surrounding vendors. She didn't look afraid. She looked like someone filing evidence in real time.

Mozart leaned against my calf then, warm and solid. His weight was grounding. His ears told a different story. They remained alert, his whole little body tense. He wasn't looking at the winged jaguar anymore. He was scanning the crowd, same as I was.

I gave his head a soft pat. "I know, bud. Something's off."

And it was. Because someone was missing.

"Where's María?" I asked softly, more to myself than to Lizzie.

She looked around, frowning. "The woman staying at our hotel? She was here?"

"She was." I searched the crowd again, then a second time. No sun-worn jacket. No quiet stillness. No telltale paper-wrapped package.

Nothing.

"She was watching him earlier," I murmured. "Locked in on him."

"And now she's gone?" Lizzie asked, voice pitched low. "That's not shady at all."

It wasn't really. There could have been a million reasons she had left the *mercado*. If you asked me, it *was* telling. Because amid the chaos and flashing lights and whispered speculation, one thing was certain. The killer hadn't just left their mark on Curtis Vale.

They'd left a ripple in every person standing there.

And María? It didn't look like she was ready to be caught in it.

We left the *mercado* in silence. It felt like anything we would have said wouldn't make a difference just yet.

The path back to the hotel was uneven and hushed, lit only by twinkling paper lanterns and the occasional streetlamp. Even the marigolds seemed quieter now, petals curling slightly at the edges as if the whole city had exhaled and was trying to forget what it had seen.

Mozart padded along beside me, leash slack between us, his nose occasionally brushing the cobblestones like he was still tracking whatever emotional scent hung in the air. Lizzie walked on my other side, unusually subdued.

"That winged jaguar," she finally said, voice low. "It's cursed. It has to be."

I didn't respond right away. The image of the body—slumped just so, draped against the carving like some macabre installation—kept cycling through my head. The light catching the curve of the paint. The odd stillness. The precision.

It hadn't felt accidental.

I thought about María—how still she'd stood across the plaza, her eyes locked on Vale like he was the final page in a story only she knew the beginning of. And then gone, vanished into the tide of tourists and twilight. I thought about the man with the lined face and haunted jaw, holding Catalina like he was the only thing keeping her upright. I thought about the way Curtis Vale had raised that glass of *mezcal* like the crowd owed him a toast.

And then I thought about where he'd ended up.

"That wasn't just murder," I said quietly, more to myself than to Lizzie.

She looked over at me, eyes searching.

"That was a statement."

We walked the last block in silence, the only sound of Mozart's paws on stone and the soft rustle of *papel picado* overhead. It fluttered in the warm breeze like it was trying to warn us.

I didn't know what the message was, even though someone in this city had tried to make sure it was delivered loud and clear. With Curtis Vale as the punctuation mark.

* * *

SUNRISE FOUND us in the courtyard of *Casa de las Bugambilias,* surrounded by blooming bougainvillea and the unsettling quiet that follows something awful.

The coffee was strong enough to rewire my central nervous system, and the *pan de muerto,* bread of the dead—sweet, soft, and scented with orange blossom—sat on my plate looking deceptively innocent.

Lizzie looked at it suspiciously. Of course, she looked at a lot of things more suspiciously since the pickled herring in Amsterdam.

I laughed. "Try some! It's like a slightly sweet, citrusy brioche with bone-shaped decorations on top—meant to honor the dead—delicious enough to make the living stick around for seconds."

Mozart had already made three dramatic lunges at a fat beetle zigzagging across the tile, failing each time with the kind of flair that suggested it was more about the game for him than any real malice.

Lizzie, wrapped in a borrowed shawl and wearing sunglasses that could block solar flares, chewed her bread like it might confess something if she gave it long enough.

The courtyard should have been buzzing—travelers trading restaurant tips, someone loudly insisting their room didn't have enough towels, kids dribbling juice down their shirts while Mozart plotted how to "accidentally" steal their breakfast. The opposite was true. It was quiet.

Too quiet.

A group of guests sat huddled near the fountain, whispering in low tones. The woman at the front desk repeated the same three phrases every few minutes, like a glitching hospitality robot.

"*Sí, es cierto.* Yes, it's true."

"*Todavía no.* No, they haven't caught anyone."

"*No era famoso.* He wasn't famous."

I broke off a piece of bread and gave it to Mozart, who sniffed it first—as if to check for spiritual residue—before accepting it like a prince being hand-fed.

Lizzie sipped her coffee, then muttered behind her mug, "Tell me this isn't giving you flashbacks to that time in China."

"The one where the opera singer got skewered with a ceremonial *jian*?"

"Like a cheese cube on a charcuterie board." She sighed. "Good lord. We've done this too many times."

"Mm," I hummed because I wasn't ready to admit she was right.

A pair of teenage girls walked past us whispering in rapid Spanish, casting nervous glances toward the street. One of them clutched a souvenir sugar skull to her chest like it might ward off whatever bad spirits were still drifting around the plaza.

I didn't believe in curses. I did believe in timing. And someone had chosen last night's moment with surgical precision.

I hadn't meant to eavesdrop. In my defense, the courtyard was quiet, the coffee was almost gone, and the only other conversation happening was between Mozart and the beetle he still hadn't caught.

Two women sat at the next table, both in embroidered blouses and chunky bracelets that clicked softly when they gestured. Local, by the sound of their Spanish—soft, fast, musical. A language not meant for tourists.

"Fue un trato grande," one said, lowering her voice even though there was no one within five feet. A big deal.

"Con alguien importante," the other replied. With someone important.

I leaned just a bit to the side under the guise of brushing croissant flakes off my lap.

"Navarro," one of them said.

The other nodded, looking around like the plants might be listening.

Then: *"Y Don Abel..."* Her voice dropped further, just a breath. *"Él sabía."*

He knew.

Navarro. Don Abel. The name on the fire-damaged shop. Something tightened at the back of my throat. I didn't know what the connection was. My instincts stirred like a dog catching the scent of rain on dry air.

Lizzie leaned in, pretending to reapply lip balm. "You're getting that look again."

"What look?"

"The one that means we're not going sightseeing today."

I ignored her and kept listening.

"Se suponía que eso quedara enterrado," one whispered.

It was supposed to stay buried.

They stood a few minutes later and drifted toward the front lobby, their bracelets whispering secrets all the way out.

I stared at the last crumbs of my bread, suddenly dry on my tongue.

Mozart nudged my knee with his snout and licked his lips. Lizzie slid her plate toward him without breaking eye contact.

"Well?" she asked. "What are we digging up this time?"

"I'm not sure yet," I said, still staring at the path the

women had taken. "Whatever it is… I'm starting to get the feeling it wasn't meant to be uncovered."

I was still turning over the phrase supposed to stay buried when Mozart struck.

One second, Lizzie's toast sat perfectly untouched beside her coffee. The next, there was a blur of fur, a small thud, and Mozart triumphantly trotting two feet away with a whole slice of *pan tostado* clutched between his teeth.

"Mozart!" Lizzie yelped, nearly sloshing her café con leche down the front of her blouse. "Bring that back! It was artisanal!"

Mozart settled under the wrought iron bench with the stealth of a jewel thief, tail thumping like this had been the plan all along.

"He's a dog of discerning palate," I said, trying not to smile. "You did leave it unattended."

"I looked away for three seconds!"

"That's more than enough time for a seasoned thief." I dropped a napkin to the floor, then crouched down to retrieve it. "Or an investigator with excellent instincts."

Mozart gave me a crumb-covered wink. Probably accidental. Eerily well-timed.

Lizzie crossed her arms. "That toast had mango marmalade."

I gave her a sympathetic nod. "He honors the dead by stealing their carbs."

"Rude."

"I didn't say it wasn't."

Still kneeling, I caught sight of the newspaper folded neatly on the service table by the coffee carafe—today's *El Sol de Oaxaca. The Sun of Oaxaca*. A blurry photo of the plaza was splashed across the front page, the winged jaguar *alebrije* lit by flashbulbs and lanterns, a red-and-yellow blur of police tape in the foreground.

I stood and reached for it, the weight of the paper oddly heavy in my hands.

"Here," I said, holding it out. "Instead of toast."

Lizzie narrowed her eyes. "This better have a horoscope."

"It has something better."

Because even before I opened it, I had a feeling this morning's headlines weren't going to be about the festival anymore.

I unfolded the paper and skimmed past the bold headline—something about tragedy, tourism, and the importance of respecting sacred spaces. The subhead added, "Authorities believe it was an accident. Locals are not so sure."

Mozart rested his chin on my foot like he agreed with the latter.

The photo stretched across the front page: the winged jaguar alebrije illuminated in dramatic contrast, surrounded by police tape and silhouettes of onlookers. The camera flash had caught the paint's metallic glint, giving the carved beast an eerie glow, like it was watching the chaos it had unwittingly—or not—become part of.

Lizzie leaned in. "Is that us in the background? Oh my god. Do I look concerned or constipated?"

"Neither," I murmured, already tuning her out.

Because something else had caught my eye.

In the lower right-hand corner of the photo—partially cropped, barely visible—was a crate. On top of it sat a carving. Small, dark, detailed. The pattern along its back was familiar: swirling lines in a style I'd seen before. Not just anywhere.

Yesterday. When Vale—Curtis Vale, I now knew—had been hovering near the vendor stall, camera out and charm on high, he'd been circling a display of similar carvings. This one stood out... this one had something different. The shape of the jaw. The slope of the spiral tail. The wings. It wasn't just similar. It was one of those carvings.

Or a match to it.

And that meant either Vale had been near that crate earlier in the day—or someone had moved it into frame later, after the body had been discovered.

"Look at this," I said, tapping the edge of the photo.

Lizzie squinted. "What am I looking at?"

"That carving."

"Okay?"

"I've seen it before. It wasn't there last night. Not when we first arrived."

She looked at me like I'd announced I could speak to the marigolds.

"You're telling me you remember one specific jaguar carving out of, like, a thousand?"

"I'm telling you it's the same one Vale was circling when he got into it with that other guy. Molina."

Lizzie raised an eyebrow. "So, it walked into frame by itself?"

"Or someone wanted it seen."

Mozart gave a soft whuff, like he was offering moral support or objecting to the idea that statues could move on their own.

I stared down at the photo again, my thumb resting on the edge of the crate.

Something about the angle. The placement. It wasn't just background noise—it was deliberate.

"Whoever staged that shot," I said quietly, "wanted us to notice the carving. And now I can't stop wondering why."

Lizzie took the paper from my hands and tilted it slightly, squinting at the photo again like it might rearrange itself under scrutiny.

"So," she said slowly, "you're saying either someone

moved the carving after the body was found... or it was already there and we missed it?"

"I don't miss things," I said. "You know that."

"I do. Which is why I'm officially creeped out."

She turned the paper upside down and stared at it like she was checking for hidden messages. "Maybe it's cursed. Maybe the carving wanted to be seen. Like some *Día de los Muertos* version of a haunted influencer."

I arched my brow. "You're suggesting the statue staged its own press shot?"

"I'm not not suggesting it."

Mozart yawned dramatically at our feet, rolled onto his back, and gave the world his belly like a sacrifice.

I leaned back in my chair, looking up at the sky. The morning clouds were starting to thin. The air still held that strange weight—like a door between worlds had been nudged open, just enough to make things weird.

Lizzie folded the paper in half and tapped it against her knee.

"They say the dead come back to visit during this time of year," she said, quieter now. "What if this guy—Vale—wasn't on the invitation list?"

I looked at her.

She shrugged. "You said it yourself. It felt like a message. A warning."

"It did."

I picked up my coffee, now lukewarm and bitter, and stared into it like it might offer clarity.

"He pushed into a world that didn't want him," I said. "Took too much. Asked too few questions."

"And someone made sure he got an answer."

Mozart sneezed, then curled up in a satisfied doughnut on Lizzie's shawl.

"Do me a favor," Lizzie said, "and if we find out that carving has a name, don't say it out loud."

"Deal."

In the back of my mind, though, I knew that whatever the carving represented—whoever had carved it, moved it, placed it—wasn't finished speaking. And I was ready to listen.

The courtyard had emptied out except for us and a few other guests, lingering over their coffee with that same distracted air I'd seen after press conferences and breakups—when people know something big has happened but can't decide if they're supposed to be part of it.

Mozart stirred beside me, lifting his head briefly before letting out a sigh that said he was officially done with breakfast drama and death for the morning.

I envied him.

Lizzie had disappeared inside to find stronger coffee—or possibly a croissant that hadn't been spiritually compromised—and I was left staring at the folded newspaper in my lap.

I turned it over one more time, scanning the background of the photo again. Looking past the carving at the other details. Crates. Shadows. Shapes that didn't mean anything yet. Instinct told me they might.

I didn't know exactly what I was looking for. That tug in my gut was one I'd come to recognize—the feeling when a thread was waiting to be pulled. There was something in that shot that wasn't random. A story behind the shape of the carving. A pattern I hadn't deciphered yet.

And then there was María—gone before the body hit the gossip circuit. Gerardo Molina, calculating. Catalina, shaken. The man with the carved hands and the heavy eyes. Dr. Pineda, still and watching like she was waiting for someone to ask the right question.

If only I knew what the question was. I sighed. I folded

the paper slowly and set it down beside me. Mozart nudged my ankle with his nose.

"Yeah," I murmured. "I feel it too."

I looked toward the courtyard gate, where the city beyond was beginning to stir again—horns honking, vendors setting up, the smell of roasted chilies already curling into the air. Somewhere out there was a killer. And the longer I sat with it, the more I knew. They didn't kill Curtis Vale to hide the truth.

They killed him to wake it up.

MASKS AND MOTIVES

The market had reinvented itself.

Gone were the hushed whispers and police tape. In their place: *papel picado* flapping joyfully overhead, drums echoing off the stone, and a crowd thick with sugar skulls and sunscreen. You'd never guess someone had died violently beneath a ten-foot winged jaguar carving just hours before.

Well. Violently and tastefully. It had flair, if nothing else.

Mozart trotted ahead with purpose, sniffing each food stall like a customs dog with a flare for the dramatic. He paused at a candle-lit altar stacked with *tamales* and promptly tried to eat someone's ancestor's offering.

"Respect the dead," I muttered, tugging his leash gently. "Or at least don't chew on their lunch."

Lizzie was already ten stalls ahead, wrapped in a gauzy pink shawl that made her look like a Day of the Dead fairy godmother. She had a flower crown in her hair and glitter on her cheekbones. I tried to stay in step. My mind kept drifting back to the winged jaguar statue.

The carving style, sure—and the look of it. The colors, the

spirals, the way the red had bled through the carved grooves after Curtis Vale's body slumped against it. The image had lodged in my brain like a splinter. Not gruesome. Not even sad. Just wrong. Deliberate.

Mozart pulled again, this time toward a stall selling painted skulls and carved hearts, each one more ornate than the last. I let him lead, my gaze skipping over painted gourds and embroidered sashes, waiting for something—anything—to catch the same frequency as that spiraled winged jaguar.

"Festival energy is everything," Lizzie said as she reappeared beside me, now inexplicably carrying a small skeletal *Mariachi* figurine. "It's giving me life. And possibly cavities."

"I can feel the joy radiating off you."

"You know I process trauma through glitter and snacks. You should try it."

I raised a brow. My lips stayed closed. Mozart sneezed once and trotted forward, tail flicking like a metronome.

As we rounded a corner, the music shifted—drums replaced by plucked guitar and a chorus of children laughing behind bright painted masks. Their faces were foxes, owls, deer, and rabbits—all hand-carved, all smiling, all just slightly off.

Masks that watched you back.

I paused, arms crossed, heart tugging toward something just out of reach. The mood had shifted again, subtly, like a dancer slipping between steps. The city was dancing. I couldn't help wondering to whose rhythm?

Suddenly, I thought I caught sight of María darting across the *mercado*. She carried something small, tucked under her arm. I wondered briefly if she had reclaimed her lost package from the airport.

"María!" I called out. She hurried on, heading toward the vendor stalls. I could have sworn she saw us.

Mozart let out a soft growl—not warning, not distress.

Just alert. And I did what I always do when the hair on my neck starts to rise. I followed it.

We were passing a booth selling painted gourds and lacquered skulls when Lizzie stopped short and let out a soft, impressed "Well, hello."

I followed her gaze. Leaning casually against a stone planter just off the main path—one hand resting on a red cane, the other holding a cigar between thick fingers—stood a man straight out of central casting for "Retired But Still Respected." Bowling shirt, heavy gold watch, pressed slacks, the kind of hat that said he'd walked through storms and come out the other side dry. He wasn't working in a stall. He wasn't buying either.

He was surveying.

Like the whole market was a kingdom and someone had just died without asking permission.

"That's the guy," Lizzie whispered, adjusting her shawl like it was armor. "From last night. The one Vale called Molina."

Molina. No first-name necessary. He didn't look like the kind of man who appreciated familiarity.

"You're not actually going to—" I started. Lizzie was already peeling away. She approached with the kind of easy confidence that got her upgrades in airports and second drinks on the house.

"Excuse me," she said warmly. "That hat? *Muy caliente.*"

I winced. Great. In the entire language, *that's* the phrase she knows.

"I had to say so," she continued. "You've got presence."

Gerardo turned slowly. He took in her compliment, her grin, her glitter-dusted cheekbones—then gave the world's smallest nod. Respect acknowledged, not returned.

"You American?" he asked, cigar still in hand.

"Most of the time," Lizzie said. "We travel a lot. Out to

appreciate the world. Art, culture… the real stuff. Not the tourist fluff."

That got a faint smirk. Barely.

"He didn't come to appreciate it," he said, not bothering to clarify who.

I stepped in before Lizzie could fish too deep in one cast.

"Curtis Vale?" I asked.

Molina looked at me like he already knew the answer and was wondering if I had the spine to follow it through.

"He came to steal," he said simply. "To take patterns that aren't his. Techniques passed down by hand and memory. Copy them. Flatten them. Sell them to people who don't know the difference—and don't care."

"Cheap knockoffs," I said quietly.

Molina exhaled, smoke curling from his mouth like punctuation. "Not knockoffs. Homages."

He let the word hang for a moment. Then, with a shrug, almost as an afterthought:

"You sell one or two to the right gallery, it's a celebration of folk heritage. You sell a thousand to tourists out of a catalog, and suddenly everyone's got an opinion."

There it was. A slip. He didn't hate what Vale was doing. He hated how he was doing it.

Lizzie shifted, her voice softer now. "Someone made sure he couldn't do it again."

Molina didn't blink. Didn't nod. Just looked at us with the expression of a man who'd already made his peace with fire and wasn't afraid to watch something else burn.

He tapped the ash from his cigar, turned, and walked away into the crowd.

Mozart, sitting at my feet, let out a low exhale. Like even he knew that was the kind of man who didn't say things he didn't mean.

Lizzie turned to me slowly. "I'd ask what that was. I'm afraid the answer might curse my coffee, though."

"He was telling us a story," I said. "One he didn't want his name on."

"And Vale?"

I looked out across the festival crowd, where masks and flowers danced beside smiling skeletons.

"He tried to rewrite it."

Mozart tugged me toward a row of booths just off the main drag, where the music faded slightly and the shadows stretched longer. Lizzie had veered off again, this time lured by a stand of dancing skeleton marionettes, so it was just me and the world's nosiest Schnoodle on a mission.

That's when I saw them.

A stall draped in bright fabric and dangling paper flags, the front lined with a perfect row of jaguar figurines. Each one different. Each one fierce.

Some were playful, almost cartoonish—wide grins, swirling colors, stylized ears. Others...others were something else entirely.

Hand-carved. Wood, aged and polished, with layers of paint so vibrant they looked almost wet. The patterns coiled like smoke—lightning on the cheeks, lashes of red across the snout, gold teeth tucked behind snarling lips. And one of them—

One of them looked back.

I stepped closer.

It wasn't just similar to the *alebrije* from last night. It was it—at least in spirit. Spiraled eyes, crimson-tipped fangs, a curve to the cheekbone that struck a chord I hadn't even known was playing. The spiral pattern along its brow danced if you stared too long. Like it was daring you to forget where you'd seen it.

It was the jaguar from the crime scene—translated into

smaller form. Still unmistakable. Same rage. Same elegance. Same quiet menace. Wings and all.

Mozart sat beside me, unmoving, nose twitching. Watching it too.

I reached out, not to touch it, just to hover near the edge of the figure's jawline.

There was power in it. Not magic exactly. Not superstition. Just weight. The kind of weight that came with memory —and, lately, with death.

The vendor noticed me staring and shuffled over.

"Do you know who made this one?" I asked in Spanish.

She looked at the winged jaguar figurine, then back at me. And for a moment, her whole posture shifted—shoulders tensing, gaze widening as all the color drained from her face.

"That is not mine," she rushed, mumbling something else in hushed Spanish and crossing herself. Her eyes darted nervously. "That is the Navarro style. Died out after the fire." She snatched it from my hands. "Someone is playing a cruel joke."

And just like that, I felt the first real shiver at the base of my spine.

I apologized and stepped back, the weight of her words following me like the smoke curling from the altar stalls.

Died out after the fire.

The winged jaguar figure I'd just seen didn't look like something that had died. It looked reborn. Repainted. Reclaimed. The lines were too fresh, the hand too confident.

And if it matched the *alebrije* from the crime scene, then maybe someone was still making work in that forbidden style—quietly, maybe, but intentionally. Like a signature scratched into the wood with a secret no one wanted spoken aloud.

Mozart trotted ahead, then doubled back, sneezing loudly

at a cone of smoldering copal. He gave the burner an offended sniff and looked up at me, ears twitching.

"I know," I said, flipping open my notebook as we moved away from the stall. "Something smells off."

I clicked my pen and scrawled the words across a fresh page.

Style. Pattern. Burned. Not lost?

Mozart pressed against my leg, warm and steady. A nudge. A vote. Agreement.

Something had been brought back that was never supposed to return. And someone, somewhere, had decided to make it visible again.

Lizzie caught up to me near a stall selling blown-glass hummingbirds, her arms now full of things I was certain wouldn't survive airport security.

"There you are," she said, squinting at my expression. "You've got the look."

"What look?"

"The one that means you've either found a clue or communed with the dead."

I didn't answer. I was still thinking about the spirals. The fangs. The way the vendor's whole body had reacted when I said Navarro without actually saying anything.

"You know that winged jaguar I was staring at?" I asked.

"The one with the murder energy?"

"It matches the *alebrije* from the crime scene. Same pattern. Same spiral motif. Same everything."

Lizzie's brow lifted. "That's not the kind of coincidence we like."

"No," I agreed. "It's the kind we investigate."

We wandered down a narrower alleyway between booths, Mozart sniffing along the base of a clay display like he was looking for a secret door. A trio of older women in *rebozos*, shawls, stood huddled near a tamarind vendor, talking softly in Spanish. I caught one word clearly.

Navarro.

I slowed. Lizzie, sensing a shift, fell silent beside me.

The women's voices dropped even lower. The name came again—threaded into phrases I only half caught. "The old fire… the daughter…" and something about *"El taller perdido."* The lost workshop.

Then one of them glanced our way, and instantly broke apart. A scattering of movement, as if they'd remembered they were being watched.

Lizzie sighed. "That's never a good sign."

"No," I said. "It *can* be a useful one."

I jotted the name down in my notebook, underlined it twice.

Navarro.

It wasn't just a name anymore. It was a shadow stretching forward from a fire everyone pretended was long gone—and a style someone was still trying to resurrect. I finally had the right question to ask.

Who was Navarro?

Now, I just needed to find the right someone to ask.

I didn't expect the first vendor to answer. He was an older man, his hands stained with dye and time, bent over a basket of woven bands that shimmered like desert heat. I crouched beside Mozart, pretended to be interested in a sash, and asked—gently—"Do you know anything about Navarro?"

He didn't look up. Just said, "No," too quickly. Too flatly.

Second attempt. A woman arranging tiny sugar figurines in neat rows, her eyes sharp beneath her headscarf. I bought two skulls, complimented the detail work, and asked the same question.

She smiled politely. "We don't speak of old fires."

I thanked her, even as my skin prickled.

Third time. A young artisan sketching with charcoal on the back of a receipt book, her stall stacked with clay whistles shaped like hummingbirds. Her hands paused mid-line when I said the name.

Then she shook her head. "Too long ago," she said. "No one remembers."

Her knuckles were white on the paper. They all remembered. They just didn't want to. Mozart let out a huff as we walked on, the market now feeling less festive, more watchful. The color hadn't drained from the day. Something else had. Openness. Ease.

"They've built walls around the story," I said quietly.

Lizzie bit into a guava candy, chewing with a frown. "Maybe to keep people out."

"Or to keep something in."

And if that was the case, I intended to pry the first brick loose.

Back at the hotel, the courtyard felt deceptively calm. A breeze played with the bougainvillea. Somewhere, someone was grinding beans for the afternoon coffee service. Lizzie had vanished upstairs with her haul like a dragon nesting on festival trinkets.

Mozart flopped under the table with a dramatic sigh and all four paws in the air, blissfully unaware that his morning of sleuthing had unearthed something bigger than either of us could explain yet.

I pulled out the copy of *El Sol de Oaxaca* we'd grabbed earlier and laid it flat across the table. The photograph from the crime scene still dominated the front page—winged jaguar *alebrije* lit from beneath, its carved spiral eyes seeming to glow even in print.

I reached for my notebook and clipped the photo onto a fresh page.

Then, next to it, I sketched the giant winged jaguar figure

from the square. Just the details that stuck in memory—the fang tilt, the spiral pattern, the brushstroke curves that weren't quite symmetrical but still felt intentional.

Beside that, the smaller winged jaguar I'd seen near the edge of the market. Smaller, but speaking the same visual language. I didn't need to be fluent to hear what it was saying.

Style. Signature. Still alive.

Footsteps behind me. Lizzie reappeared, now without her shawl and with a cinnamon cookie in each hand. She set one in front of me without ceremony and took a bite out of the other.

"So," she said through crumbs. "Who's making the old new again?"

I didn't answer right away. I looked down at the sketches, the photo, the names scrawled in looping ink. Vale. Navarro. María. Molina.

Lines were starting to form between them.

Mozart nudged my foot once—gentle, insistent.

"You're right," I murmured. "We're not chasing a killer."

I tapped the newspaper photo once, then closed the notebook slowly.

"We're chasing a ghost."

THE CALM BEFORE THE FALL

The cemetery looked different at night—less like a place of endings and more like a gathering space, softly breathing with memory.

Mozzie padded quietly at my side, his usual bounce subdued by the hush that blanketed the rows of headstones. Lizzie walked beside me, arms tucked into her shawl, the scent of marigolds and melting wax drifting past us like the ghost of perfume.

The vigil had already begun. *Tapetes* stretched along the cobbled paths—vibrant, intricate patterns made of colored sawdust and petals. Some had delicate skulls outlined in gold. Others bore the names of the departed, lovingly formed in loops of orange and blue. The candlelight flickered low, casting dancing shadows over everything.

We didn't speak for the first few moments. Not because we'd agreed to silence, but because it felt wrong to break it. There was music playing from somewhere deeper in the crowd. Guitar strings, slow and mournful, like the kind of song that didn't need words to get its point across.

Lizzie leaned toward me, her voice barely above a whisper.

"Is it weird I kinda love this? Like... if I had to die and be remembered, I'd want it to look like this. Preferably with a better headshot."

I gave her a look. The small smile that tugged at my mouth undermined the visual reprimand.

"You're not dying. You just haven't had dinner."

"Same difference," she murmured.

Still, even Lizzie—irreverent, caffeinated Lizzie—was visibly moved. Her eyes darted over the tapetes like they were sacred texts. She caught sight of a little altar set against a tree, covered in framed photos and votive candles, and for once, she didn't say a word.

Mozzie stopped to sniff at the edge of one of the tapetes near a low stone bench, his nose hovering just over a swirl of purple and green. I tugged him back gently and nodded toward the design.

"This one's Quetzalcoatl," I said softly, tracing the shape in the air with a fingertip. "The feathered serpent. See the scales here? They used dried leaves to texture the body. And those tiny red bits? That's ground chili. Not just pretty—fragrant, too."

Lizzie tilted her head, studying it like a painting.

"Whoever did that has the patience of a saint."

I nodded. "Or grief that needed a place to go."

Grief had a shape here. A color. A rhythm. It wasn't loud or messy or dramatic—it was quiet and communal, passed between hands like a lit candle. And for the first time all day, I let myself exhale fully. Nothing had been resolved, but—for just a moment—it felt like we were allowed to stand still.

Lizzie tilted her head. "Is this... like a rug?"

I smiled, just a little.

"Kind of. *Tapete* means 'carpet' in Spanish. But it's not

something you walk on. It's made with sawdust, flower petals, ash, and even seeds sometimes. Built right on the ground, just for tonight."

She squinted at it. "So... it's temporary?"

"Completely," I said. "They're meant to disappear. That's the point. You make something beautiful, pour all your love or grief into it, and then—poof. Gone by morning."

Lizzie was quiet a beat longer than usual.

"People are amazing," she finally said.

I nodded. "Especially when they know it won't last."

We continued moving slowly through the rows of headstones, the candlelight stretching long shadows that danced across our feet. The night air carried the smell of copal wood and something faintly sweet—*pan de muerto,* maybe—mingling with the dry tang of dust and marigold pollen.

Altars flanked the path like little islands of memory. Some were simple: a framed photo, a candle, a cup of hot chocolate still steaming. Others were ornate, layered with *papel picado,* candy skulls, fruit, and glowing tea lights balanced carefully along lace-draped crates.

One altar stopped me mid-step. It sat low, almost at Mozzie's eye level, built on an overturned milk crate. A child's face smiled out from a school photo—teeth uneven, eyes wide behind wire-frame glasses. Around the frame were crayon drawings folded into fans, tiny toy dinosaurs, and a half-finished coloring book. The sight of it hit me somewhere just under the ribs.

Next to it stood another altar entirely different—masculine, weathered, and proudly unvarnished. A full bottle of whiskey held court beside a deck of worn domino tiles arranged in a half-played game. A cigar rested in a ceramic ashtray shaped like a crawfish. Whoever he was, he had a sense of humor.

Mozzie sniffed near the dominoes, maintained a

respectful curiosity. I gave his leash a light tug anyway, not wanting him to disturb anything sacred.

Lizzie didn't say a word. She just slid her hand into the crook of my elbow and squeezed once. No joke. No commentary. Just presence.

I let my shoulders drop. The tension that had hitched itself to me since sunrise finally loosened, just a little. There was something healing about it all—the way sorrow had been shaped into something tender and bright. I didn't feel good, exactly. At least, I felt still. And that was a start.

Mozzie bumped against my leg gently, then turned, ears perking.

That's when I saw her.

Mozzie stiffened beside me, his nose twitching as he angled slightly away from the path. I followed his gaze, expecting a squirrel—or maybe someone offering tamales. His ears flattened, and before I could react, he lunged.

"Mozzie—no!" I yanked the leash. It slipped through my fingers.

He bounded forward, weaving between clusters of people and narrowly missing a low altar lined with votives. I stumbled after him, muttering apologies and ignoring the burn in my calves as I navigated uneven ground in boots that were cute but never meant for speed.

I lost sight of him for a second—just a flicker—then spotted him again near a large ofrenda lit with white candles.

And that's when he jumped. Straight up—front paws against a woman's chest like he was greeting a long-lost friend.

The woman let out a startled gasp, stumbling back a step as she tried to catch her balance. Her shawl slipped off one shoulder, and her bag swayed violently to the side. She was dressed in black, hair coiled into a braid and pinned with a deep red hibiscus. It took a second for my brain to catch up with my eyes.

María.

Mozzie yelped mid-greeting. A sharp, surprised sound.

By the time I reached them, he was back on all fours, paw curled against his chest, eyes wide and ears pinned. María was already crouching beside him, her eyes darting to see whose attention the commotion may have drawn.

I dropped to my knees beside her, breath caught somewhere between panic and suspicion.

"What happened?" I asked, reaching for Mozzie's raised paw.

María didn't answer right away. She was already examining the pad between his toes, her brow drawn. It wasn't worry. It was focus. Surgical.

"There," she murmured, more to herself than me.

She pinched something delicately between two fingers and pulled it free with a swift, practiced motion. Mozzie gave a soft whine but didn't resist. María held up the culprit: a thin, jagged sliver of red-painted wood, about the length of a matchstick. One end was splintered. The paint flaked near the tip.

"Looks like he caught himself on something," she said, her voice low and even.

"On you," I said, not accusing—just stating. "I saw him jump up."

She looked at me then. Really looked.

"I didn't see where it came from."

Before I could respond, she took my hand, turned my palm up towards her, and placed the splinter there, closing my fingers around it gently. Firmly. Her hand was warm. Dry.

"Best to keep that," she said. "In case you need to show a vet later."

And just like that, she stood. Brushed off her skirt.

"I'm actually very glad I ran into you. I have been thinking of how I could repay your kindness from the airport—letting me share the taxi with you." She smiled. "How would you like to get a local's view of *Día de los Muertos*? See firsthand how the altars are built?"

I exchanged an excited glance with Lizzie, whose eyes twinkled. My traveling companion nodded exuberantly. I turned back to María.

"That would be amazing. It would give some wonderful background information to bring my article to life. I'm writing a piece about all the fantastic food for my magazine —*The Wandering Foodie*? If I didn't highlight the rich culture the foods come from, it would be criminal!"

"Criminal?" María laughed a little too loudly, drawing a few disappointing glances from the abuelas. "Well, we can't have that, now, can we? Meet me tomorrow at *Iglesia del Espíritu Guardián*. I would love to share my heritage!"

"Looking forward to it!" I confirmed.

María gave Mozart one final pat on the head and walked away.

I stood there for a long moment after María disappeared into the crowd, still crouched beside Mozzie like I hadn't quite caught up to the moment.

My heritage. Like she wasn't just a tourist. The thought bounced around in my head like a ping pong ball.

Mozart nuzzled my arm softly, the adrenaline already gone from his body. Typical Mozzie—quick to forgive, slower to forget. I gave him a small scratch behind the ear, then opened my hand.

The splinter sat in my palm like a warning.

It was painted—a deep, faded red, the kind of color that felt old even under candlelight. The tip was jagged, almost sharp, and the paint had flaked just enough to show the grain beneath. It wasn't the kind of wood used for tapetes or altar frames. It wasn't from a bench. It wasn't from the path.

It didn't belong here.

And I couldn't explain how I knew that—I just did. The same way Mozzie had known to run to her—had known it was someone he knew.

I pulled a tissue from my pocket, wrapped the wood carefully, and tucked it deep into the lining of my coat. It didn't occur to me it might be evidence. It just didn't feel right to let it go. And because it was a little something about María's eyes, steady and unreadable, had followed me long after she'd walked away.

AN OFRENDA AND AN OMEN

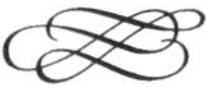

We arrived at the *Iglesia del Espíritu Guardián* just after sunrise, the sky still stretched in pale lavender and soft gold. The church sat tucked at the end of a cobbled lane, its stone façade softened by time and trumpeting bougainvillea, the bell tower silhouetted like a watchman between worlds.

María stood by the entrance arch, hair tied in a neat braid under a hoodie, which I found a little unusual. It wasn't *that* chilly.

She kept tugging at it, pulling at the stitched edges so she almost resembled a turtle who had pulled it's head into it's shell.

"I'm glad you're here," she said simply, eyes flitting down to Mozart, who wore a borrowed garland of marigolds around his neck like it was his birthright.

"Don't let the flowers fool you," I said. "He's still the same emotionally manipulative snack thief underneath."

Mozart sneezed delicately and wagged his tail, as if accepting both insult and invitation.

The courtyard unfolded behind María, shaded by jacaranda

trees and woven with the scent of incense, citrus, and bread. Long folding tables had been set up in a wide U-shape, draped in embroidered cloth and already lined with boxes of offerings —candles, fruit, framed photographs, sugar skulls so brightly painted they looked like they were grinning secrets.

Lizzie inhaled like she'd just walked into a spa made of nostalgia and color.

"Oh my gosh, it's like a garden party for ghosts," she whispered. "This is the most beautiful haunting I've ever seen."

"It's not haunting," I said, quietly. "It's homecoming."

And I meant it.

There was something reverent here. Something old and gentle and fiercely kept alive by the hands of women who remembered things others had tried to forget. Every flower, every glint of light, every crumb of *pan de muerto* placed with love and a kind of ceremonial correctness that had nothing to do with performance.

This wasn't for tourists.

This was for them. The ones who weren't here anymore —but hadn't quite left.

We were immediately adopted by a cluster of *abuelas* at the far table, who fussed over Mozart's garland, declared him "*perrito espiritual*," spirit dog, and fed him bits of sweet bread like he was a visiting saint in a fur coat. He leaned into it with the solemn dignity of a dog who understood both ceremony and carbohydrates.

Lizzie, naturally, was already elbow-deep in a box of painted votives, asking intelligent questions and managing not to knock anything over. She wore her respect like she wore her linen—light, graceful, and effortlessly appropriate.

I stayed quiet, observing. Absorbing. This was more than tradition. It was resistance. Memory made visible.

And I couldn't help but think of Curtis Vale, with his

smug smile and shutter-click entitlement, walking through a space like this with the same gaze he used for window displays and wine labels.

The courtyard filled slowly, in that unhurried, purposeful way sacred spaces do. A few of the *abuelas* pulled folding chairs into shady corners. Children arrived with arms full of baskets and sugar skulls, laughing softly as they were shushed by their mothers. Someone began humming—low and off-key and perfect—and above it all, the scent of marigolds thickened like honey in the air.

María appeared at my side with a small bundle of incense sticks and the calm of someone who belonged to the space and the silence both.

"I thought it might be good," she said, "to understand what they are building."

"I'd like that."

She led me to a table where pieces of the altar were still being assembled—its skeletal frame like the bones of a memory waiting to be fleshed out.

"There are six traditional elements placed on every *ofrenda*," she began, brushing her fingers gently over a woven cloth already set across the altar's base. "Each one is a kind of invitation."

She pointed first to the framed photographs lined up along the top tier. "*Fotos de los difuntos*—photos of our loved ones who have passed. This is how we remember who we're calling back. Their faces bring them close."

I nodded, my gaze catching on one photo: a man in a straw hat holding a carving knife and a coyote figurine. He looked both serious and amused, like he knew something you didn't. I didn't ask the name. I had a feeling I already knew.

María moved to a brass bowl in the center. It was filled

with twinkling candles—some short, some tall, all glowing in the gentle shade.

"Fire," she said simply. "*Las velas* light the way. They guide the spirits home. One for each soul you hope will return."

Mozart sat beside a dancing candle, tail still, eyes soft. His marigold garland caught the breeze and turned him briefly into something mythic.

María pointed to a bundle of *cempasúchil* blossoms—bright orange marigolds, their ruffled heads full and glowing. "These are the flowers of the dead," she said. "The scent helps guide them. We spread petals in a trail from the door to the altar. So they know the way."

Marigold petals littered the courtyard like little bursts of sun, even in the shadow.

Next came the food—bowls of mole, tamales wrapped in banana leaves, candied pumpkin, slices of *pan de muerto* with bones sculpted into the crust.

"They come hungry," she said with a smile. "And what you loved in life, you still crave in death. So we feed them. With what they loved. With what we remember."

Mozart eyed the *pan de muerto* as a young woman placed more on the table. "Sorry, Mozart. That's not for you, bud." He whimpered disappointedly.

"And these," María said, picking up a small skull from the basket beside her, "are *calaveritas de azúcar*. Sugar skulls. Brightly painted, sweet but symbolic. They remind us that death isn't scary. It's part of us. We name them for those we've lost. Sometimes for the living too, just to laugh in the face of fear."

The one she held had red spirals around the eyes and gold teeth. I tried not to think of the carving from the day before.

"And the last?" I asked.

She nodded toward a shelf where small trinkets sat in a

neat line: a tin comb, a bottle of nail polish, a battered domino set.

"*Objects personales*. Things that belonged to them. Or things they loved. Dona Rosalia—she's lived here longer than most of us have been alive, knows everyone's stories—her husband always wore rose cologne. She still sprinkles it on the altar." She gestured to a gentleman near the end of the altar. That's Señor Carrillo. His aunt smoked menthols—we light one for her every year. The things that make them who they are. Were."

Not relics. Reminders. I looked around and saw more than offerings. I saw portraits. Portraits made not of brush-strokes, but of memory—pieced together with care and tenderness and ceremony. Every item placed with purpose. Every color chosen with love. Every gesture is intimate, intentional.

Curtis Vale would have photographed this like he was documenting the party aisle at one of those big box stores.

Click. Crank out. Cash in.

He would have seen objects. This, though? This was something sacred.

"Excuse me," María suddenly said. "I just remembered something I need to take care of. See you later? Maybe at the hotel?"

"Sure," I replied. I looked up and saw Catalina across the way. When I turned to watch Maria, she had lowered her head, again pulling her hoodie round her face. Strange.

I had just stepped away to grab a fresh handful of marigold petals when I heard it.

A voice—low, raspy, not meant for me. It floated from behind one of the altar tables, where two women stood side by side stringing orange blossoms onto thin twine. Their fingers worked without pause. Their words slowed me mid-step.

"...la hija de Don Abel..."

Don Abel.

The name dropped like a pebble into my chest, quiet. Heavy. I froze, one foot in sunlight, the other still tucked beneath the shade of the tree.

"La culpa fue de ella, no del fuego."

It was her fault. Not the fire's.

I ducked slightly behind a paper fan pinned to a makeshift archway, pretending to adjust my notebook. I wasn't eavesdropping. Not exactly.

I was listening to a story that wasn't mine to hear.

Okay, fine. I was eavesdropping.

"She never should've been near that workshop," one of them continued, voice thick with the kind of bitterness that ages with you. "He lost everything. His name, his hands... now his wife. And now this."

This? What was *this*?

The second woman clucked her tongue. "It is almost too much for one man to bear."

I peeked out and caught a glimpse of the first woman. Short hair. Worn cotton blouse. Her mouth was tight. Eyes sharper than her age should've allowed.

They quickly paused as someone passed behind them, then continued stringing orange blossoms in silence.

I stepped back into the courtyard and scanned the space until my eyes landed on Catalina.

She had walked past the gossiping women to stand at the far end of the table, arranging candles into a careful row. Her jaw was set. Her shoulders tense. Her whole posture screamed tension disguised as purpose.

I stared at her a little too long.

Was *she* Don Abel's daughter? His *hija*? The one, it would seem, everyone blamed for the charred remains of Don Abel Navarro's workshop?

It made sense. She was guarded, meticulous, defensive even in silence. She had snapped at Curtis Vale in the *mercado*. And everyone in the plaza seemed to watch her out of the corner of their eyes. I needed to confirm.

"Darcy."

María's voice slid in beside me, calm and measured. She was holding a shallow clay bowl filled with salt, a protective element to be added near the altar's base.

"You alright?" she asked.

"Fine," I lied, brushing a marigold petal off my sleeve. "Just… thinking."

About fires. About blame. About the way silence sometimes speaks louder than an accusation.

I watched Catalina light a match, holding it steady until the flame caught the wick of a candle. Her hand didn't even shake. Something in her face? Something there looked scorched.

"Um, I just remembered. I need to go help one of the abuelas. I'll be back." María excused herself and quickly wound her way through the crowd.

"Okay," I answered, distracted. I was still focused on Catalina. She didn't look up. I watched her a while longer anyway.

The way she smoothed the altar cloth. The intended spacing of each votive. The quiet choreography of someone who needed control in a space that was built on memory and loss.

She was good at it—almost too good. Careful and experienced.

I thought back to the night Curtis Vale's body was found —how she'd stood frozen in the mercado while Don Abel held her in place with one arm around her shoulders. It hadn't been comfort. It had been… ownership. Or maybe containment. It was hard to tell who he'd been protecting.

"Do you need help with that section?" I asked, approaching with a handful of marigolds and a disarming smile.

Catalina glanced up just long enough to take my measure, then returned to the altar. "No. Thank you."

Polite on paper. Frosted in delivery.

"You've placed everything with real care," I offered.

"It's not for display," she said, arranging a row of salt lines beneath a photograph of a small boy. "It's for them."

There was substance behind that word. Them. The ones no longer here. The ones who came back anyway.

My gaze drifted to her hands—fingertips stained red with paint, a nick on the thumb, the kind of wear that came from work involving tools and time. The same hands that had clutched an alebrije to her chest just days ago, teeth bared at Curtis Vale.

The same hands that might have pushed a man to his death.

"You and Don Abel… you work together?" I asked casually.

Her head turned just slightly, not quite enough to face me.

"He's my father," she said.

And just like that, something in my gut clicked. Of course, she was his daughter. The way he stood next to her at the *mercado*. The way he held her. The way he kept one eye on everyone else, like the past was a smoldering ember that might flare to life again at any second.

A daughter, a workshop, a fire long ago… and a father who might have feared that his daughter was a raging fire he could not control.

It made too much sense. Maybe that's why I didn't question it. Not then.

I turned to say something to Lizzie—probably a remark

about how I was single-handedly redefining the phrase emotional landmine—but I stopped when I caught sight of María.

She stood just at the edge of the courtyard entrance. Her eyes were on Catalina. It wasn't judgment. It wasn't curiosity, either. It was something quieter. Sadder. Like she was watching someone walk across a memory she hadn't expected to share.

I started walking over. When she noticed me watching, María blinked, adjusted the edge of the cloth, and stepped forward like the moment hadn't just passed through her bones.

The morning waxed on and we continued watching the altar contruction, absorbing every last detail. Lizzie negotiated her way into wrapping a candle in biodegradable gold foil (with "maximum sacred shimmer, minimal ecological guilt"), I found myself back near the center table, watching a boy no older than eight carry something small and dark in both hands like it might crumble if the wind looked at it wrong.

He moved slowly—carefully—his steps were directed by an older woman in a bright blue shawl who guided him with the kind of softness that made me ache a little. She whispered something to him in Zapotec, and he nodded once, then turned and placed the object on the altar.

A clay cup. Simple. Unglazed. Cracked along the rim. Inside it, ashes.

They caught the morning light like powdered charcoal, still laced with the faintest shimmer of something scorched long ago. Not incense. Not decorative. This was a choice. A symbol.

I turned to the woman who had guided the boy. "What does the ash mean?" I asked in Spanish.

She looked at me, then at the altar. "*Pérdida*," she said. "Loss."

Then she added, gently, "And sometimes... what we carry when the story doesn't end the way it should."

The hairs on my arms rose. I was brushing stray marigold petals off my notebook when I felt the shift in the air. Not cold. Not sharp.

Just... still.

The kind of stillness that presses on your skin before a storm—or just after someone says a name they shouldn't have.

An old woman entered the courtyard, her steps slow and stubborn, the hem of her deep purple *rebozo* trailing like a shadow behind her. She held a single object in both hands, wrapped in embroidered cloth.

Even from across the plaza, I could tell it was heavy. Her arms trembled with the effort.

The crowd hushed instinctively, like some silent chord had been struck. Even Mozart, sprawled belly-up in a patch of sun, rolled upright and watched.

The woman approached the altar in uneven steps, pausing every few feet, arms straining. Finally, the cloth slipped slightly and revealed what she carried: a sugar skull, but unlike any I'd seen that day.

It was nearly the size of a melon, dense and glossy black, painted with swirling indigo spirals that shimmered like oil on water.

A murmur passed through the crowd.

The old woman faltered, knees buckling slightly. Before I could move, Catalina appeared from the crowd like she'd been waiting for the moment.

She stepped forward quickly—no hesitation—and gently caught the edge of the skull as the woman sagged.

"I've got it," Catalina said softly, bracing the woman with one arm and reaching for the skull with the other.

The shift in weight was too sudden. The cloth slipped. The skull tilted. And then—a sound. A soft crack, like splitting bone. It wasn't much. Just a fracture down the back of the skull, no more than an inch. The snap echoed through the courtyard like a gunshot. Everyone froze.

Catalina sucked in a breath, still cradling the skull like it might fall apart in her hands. The old woman let out a whisper—"*Ay, no...*"—and covered her mouth with the edge of her *rebozo*.

A nearby abuela crossed herself.

Another muttered, "*Es un mal augurio*." A bad omen. Even the altar vibrated—as if the candles themselves had felt it.

Catalina stood rooted, her eyes fixed on the skull, now visibly fractured. She didn't cry. She didn't curse. Her jaw locked into a shape I'd seen once before—the moment before someone decides whether to tell the truth or walk away forever.

Mozart pressed against my leg and gave a low growl, almost inaudible. His ears were flat.

"I'll fix it," Catalina said finally, barely above a whisper. "I'll... try."

No one nodded. No one spoke. Because everyone knew. You can't fix what was already destroyed.

SKETCHES & SCARS

After the cracked sugar skull incident, we needed air-conditioned enlightenment and fewer omens.

The *Museo de las Culturas de Oaxaca* delivered both.

The building itself—an old Dominican monastery turned museum—rose like a sun-bleached fortress above the plaza, its stone walls thick with silence and centuries. Lizzie and I stepped through the heavy doors and into a hush that settled over our shoulders like a cool shawl. Even Mozart, tucked discreetly in his sling, seemed to understand this was not the place for expressive snorts.

We wandered through open-air corridors and cloistered walkways, every arch casting long shadows that made the light feel older somehow. The first few exhibits held sacred artifacts—Zapotec funerary urns, centuries-old codices, fragments of carved stelae worn smooth by time.

"I feel underdressed," Lizzie whispered, peering at a ceremonial headdress made of turquoise and quetzal feathers.

Mozart sneezed quietly. I wasn't sure if it was reverence or dust.

Eventually, we found our way into the folk art gallery,

tucked in one of the upper wings with a sweeping view of the botanical garden beyond. The room smelled faintly of wood polish and dried marigold petals—some curator's quiet nod to the season.

And that's where I saw them.

Alebrijes. Dozens of them, displayed in glass cases like sleeping familiars.

Some were whimsical—rabbits with wings, frogs with antlers, fish caught mid-flight. Others were darker—coyotes with spiral eyes, serpents with too many teeth, hybrid creatures twisted in impossible contortions that felt more dream than design.

I stepped closer to one of the older pieces—wood darkened with age, paint faded but still defiant—and my breath caught.

The tail curled in a familiar swirl.

Not identical to the winged jaguar from the plaza. This one didn't have wings. It still looked close. Cousins, maybe. Or echoes.

"Are you seeing this?" I asked Lizzie, who had already moved on to the next case and was pointing at something with the wingspan of a turkey.

"Huh?" she said. "Oh, yeah. Spirals. Very you."

"I'm serious."

I reached into my bag for my notebook, flipping to the sketch I'd drawn back at the hotel. Side-by-side, they hummed with shared ancestry. Different artists, maybe. That style—that rhythm in the carving, that bold tension in the line work—wasn't a coincidence.

"Navarro family," said a voice behind us. "You're seeing their signature."

We turned to find Dr. Soledad Pineda, arms folded, expression unreadable. She wasn't wearing her NGO name tag today, but she still had the posture of a woman who could politely dismantle you in a UNESCO committee meeting.

"Families of artisans," she continued, stepping beside me, "often develop what we call estilo propio—a personal style passed down through generations. The brushstrokes, the carving technique, even the pattern symmetry. It's as recognizable as a surname. Sometimes more so."

"So like... artistic DNA?" Lizzie asked.

Dr. Pineda's mouth twitched in what might have been a smile. "Exactly."

She lingered at the display case like someone visiting a shrine. Her fingers didn't touch the glass. Her posture leaned forward slightly, reverent.

"These," she said softly, "are from the Navarro family workshop. Before the fire."

I turned from the coyote carving. "Don Abel's family?"

She nodded. "Once considered the finest carvers in Arrazola. Their style was... unmistakable. Fearless. There were collectors who waited years for a single piece."

Her tone wasn't just admiration—it was the kind of melancholy that clings to something that can't be remade.

"The fire changed everything," she continued. "It destroyed the original workshop. His wife passed only a few weeks ago, but she had been little more than a hollow shell since the fire. Grief can rot you from the inside out, especially when it's mixed with blame. And Don Abel..." She hesitated. "He tried to go in. To save someone."

"Someone?" I echoed.

Dr. Pineda's eyes stayed on the jaguar. "His daughter."

I blinked. "Catalina?"

Her mouth twitched—not quite a smile. "No. His firstborn. Her name was Lucía."

I stilled.

"She was the one with the gift," Soledad said. "Young, but already carving things people twice her age couldn't dream of. Some said she had the old magic in her hands."

I glanced at the swirling tail pattern again. That same rhythm echoed in the plaza *alebrije*. My stomach tightened.

"And Don Abel hasn't carved since?"

"No," she said. "He saved the body. The price was his hands. The burns ruined them. Even if they hadn't..." She looked at me. "You can't carve when your soul's splintered. And his was."

Soledad Pineda fell silent, her eyes drifting back to the display case. Her hand, almost unconsciously, moved to her right index finger. She rubbed at the base of it, the skin red and slightly swollen. The nail was short, uneven, like it had been bitten or broken and never quite healed right.

"Are you alright?" I asked.

She blinked like she'd forgotten I was there. "Oh. Just a splinter," she answered. "Hazard of the job, sometimes. Working with these old pieces."

She said it lightly, but kept pressing the spot like it still burned.

We left a few minutes later. The image stuck with me—her finger, raw and restless, worrying at something invisible just beneath the skin.

And I found myself wondering...

Some people carried their grief like weight. Others wore it like armor. Dr. Pineda, though? She carried hers like a match still lit. And fire always leaves a scar. I wasn't sure if hers was from loss. Or revenge.

Mozart sat beside me, unusually quiet.

"So, Catalina didn't learn the family style?" I asked, still trying to stitch together what little I knew.

Soledad let out a slow breath. "She tried. Don Abel

couldn't bring himself to pass it down. He locked it away with Lucía's memory. Catalina had to teach herself."

That silence again. Not pity. Not scorn. Just the quiet that comes when grief runs out of words.

"She's not her sister," Soledad said finally. "She never will be."

I didn't know why, but the words stung on Catalina's behalf.

Before I could thank her, Dr. Pineda's gaze drifted to another case—empty, save for a small placard that read:

Pieza robada, en proceso de recuperación.

Stolen piece. In process of recovery.

Her jaw tightened.

That was odd. I looked closer at the placard.

Yaguar.

My brow arched high. Well, you didn't have to speak Spanish to figure that one out.

A sudden pop of light illuminated the room. Dr. Pineda wheeled on her heel where a couple of red-faced, sunburned tourists were snapping photos of the display cases.

"Don't they know the flash is just going to bounce off the glass?" Lizzie harrumphed, her photojournalist sensibilities offended.

"Excuse me!" Dr. Pineda interrupted the tourists. "*Está prohibido tomar fotos*. Photos aren't allowed!"

THEY APOLOGIZED in hurried midwestern accents and shuffled along to the next installment. The doctor returned to us, shaking her head. "*¡Estos condenados turistas!* Damned tourists."

"Let me guess," Lizzie said, stepping beside me. "Curtis Vale spent a lot of time here?"

Soledad Pineda didn't smile.

"He was always there," she said, voice like a blade wrapped in velvet. "At the galleries. At the festivals. Camera in hand, grin like a game show host, pretending to care."

I glanced at the plaque. "He stole from the museum?"

"Not directly," she said. "He was too clever for that." She paused, like she was considering. "At least not like that. He took ideas. Styles. Snapped photos of techniques passed down through generations and repackaged them for buyers who didn't know better. Or worse—didn't care."

Her voice lowered a register. "He called it curation."

Mozart let out a low growl, as if even he didn't buy that spin.

"Every time we caught him, he disappeared for a while. Changed distributors. Rebranded." She folded her arms. "The damage was always the same. Cheap knockoffs flooding markets, undercutting real artisans. And the elders? The ones who carved for meaning, not money? They stopped trusting anyone."

I watched her for a long moment.

Dr. Soledad Pineda, champion of cultural preservation. Cool. Composed. I could see that behind the mask, there was fire.

We thanked Dr. Pineda and stepped out of the museum and into a wall of dry heat and sharper questions.

The street outside had shifted since we'd gone in—buses coughing down the lane, a flute player outside the gates weaving something mournful into the breeze. Mentally, I was still back there, in the cool hush of the folk art gallery, staring at spirals etched by a girl who died too young… and whose patterns somehow weren't finished yet.

As we stepped into the blinding sunlight, Lizzie glanced around at the shuttered stalls and emptying streets.

. . .

"Ah yes," she said. "Almost time for *siesta*. The blessed Oaxacan tradition of pretending the world doesn't exist between tortilla time and tamale time. I unequivocally approve."

"If we hurry, we've got just enough time to talk to Catalina before everything closes up. Come on. Let's hustle."

Mozart trotted beside me, tail up, marigold garland slightly wilted but still hanging on. Lizzie walked just ahead, sunglasses on, chewing something probably smuggled out of the museum gift shop.

"She's good," I finally spoke.

"Catalina?" Lizzie asked.

I nodded. "Better than Soledad gives her credit for."

Lizzie looked sideways at me. "You think she's the one still carving the Navarro style?"

I didn't answer right away.

I thought about the winged jaguar in the plaza. The spiral skull. "She's not just good," I commented. "She's deliberate. And it sounds like she's had to fight for every inch."

"She certainly fought with Vale," Lizzie recalled.

"She certainly did. When he took her carving."

Lizzie tapped her temple. "And now you're wondering if she used that winged jaguar's claw to carve Curtis Vale."

I stopped at the edge of the plaza and looked down the street that led toward the artisan stalls.

"I don't want to speculate," I said.

Lizzie grinned. "You want to interrogate."

"Visit," I corrected. "Observe. Maybe ask a few questions."

"Respectfully?"

I shrugged. "Respectfully adjacent."

She linked her arm through mine. "Race you there."

Mozart barked, pulled forward, and nearly dislocated my shoulder.

And just like that, our next lead was no longer a museum whisper or a burnt legacy.

It was a stall.

And a woman who'd run out of places to hide the truth.

THE SPIRAL AND THE FLAME

We found Catalina's stall tucked at the quiet edge of the artisan sector, half-shaded beneath a tree whose fallen blossoms scattered like lavender confetti across the stone path. Her work was laid out in perfect rows—frogs, foxes, winged cats—all arranged like they belonged to the same patient, watchful family.

Catalina sat on a small stool behind the table, hunched slightly over a carving in progress. She didn't look up when we approached. Her shoulders tensed—just enough to let me know we weren't unexpected.

Lizzie, uncharacteristically gentle, let her fingers hover above a carved owl with swirling wings. "Your work's stunning," she said. "I swear this one's judging me."

Catalina's mouth twitched, a gleam of amusement. "That one does judge. She's the patron saint of bad decisions."

"Oh, then we're close friends."

I let the exchange hang, then stepped closer.

"We were hoping to ask you something," I said carefully.

Catalina didn't look up.

I continued. "About Curtis Vale."

At the name, her hand stilled. The reddish-orange-tipped brush she was holding dipped once, then stopped. She exhaled—not loud, not labored, just long. And she placed the brush down beside her palette with quiet finality.

"I knew him," she said after a beat. "For a time, anyway."

Mozart cocked his head. Lizzie blinked. I said nothing.

"I was young," Catalina went on, eyes still downcast. "Not stupid. Just… tired of being invisible. He came into the *mercado* like someone who'd already claimed the world and was offering me a corner of it."

She paused, then added with a trace of bitterness, "He listened. That was the trick."

She looked up at me then, not defensive—just tired. "He asked questions. About my family, my process. He said the boldness in my work reminded him of street murals in Oaxaca and sculpture from *Oaxaca de Juárez*—like he was drawing these imaginary lines of brilliance between me and artists I'd only ever read about."

I nodded, quietly. "He made you feel seen."

She smiled. It was the kind of smile, however, that didn't soften anything. "Worse. He made me feel chosen. Like he'd walked through hundreds of stalls and found me. Not my work. Me."

Her voice dropped, and she placed her hand—absently, maybe instinctively—over her stomach. Just for a second. Just enough for me to notice.

"I believed him," she said. "When he said he wanted to collaborate. When he said we'd build something together. I even showed him my sketchbook—things I hadn't carved yet. Concepts I was still shaping in my head."

She blinked hard and looked away.

"And then one day he was gone. No goodbye. No call.

Just… gone. And six weeks later, someone sent me a screenshot from a trade website. His name. My design. Labeled 'inspired by Mexican folk motifs.'"

I felt a pressure in my chest. A quiet, growing ache on her behalf.

"And by then," she said, voice low, "I knew better than to chase the copyright."

Mozart nosed gently at the curtain behind her table, and she reached down to still him, fingers brushing his head with a kind of automatic tenderness.

Lizzie stepped in, soft-voiced. "I'm sorry."

Catalina gave the barest nod. "I was too. For a while. Then I stopped being sorry and started being careful."

She gestured lightly to the neat rows of carvings on her table. Beautiful. Alluring. Marketable. And maybe a little caged.

Catalina glanced over her shoulder before speaking, her voice barely louder than the breeze.

"My father always warned me about men like him."

She didn't say Curtis's name. She didn't have to.

"He said charm is just a glove some people wear over a fist."

Her gaze dropped to the carving again.

"He saw Curtis once in the *mercado*. The day before the… before everything happened. They didn't speak, not that I saw. But when Papa came back, he was shaking. He wouldn't say why. Just told me, 'A man can only take so much theft before he decides something has to stop.'"

She looked up at me then, tired and tight-lipped. "At the time, I thought he meant the sketches."

Even as she said it, her voice wavered. As if maybe now… she wasn't so sure.

"Papa always said Curtis wasn't just a thief—he was

rotten. Not just on the outside, but deep. The kind of rot that spreads if you don't cut it out."

SHE SUDDENLY WRAPPED her arms around her waist—a frightened look ghosting across her features.

Mozart pushed past the curtain with a quiet huff, tail wagging like he'd just discovered something deliciously off-limits. I followed his line of sight and immediately saw it:

A jaguar.

Taller than anything on the table. Carved in thick, graceful lines from a piece of deep-hued copal wood. Unpainted, unfinished—still unmistakably alive. Its stance was proud, almost mid-prowl, like it had caught the scent of something and was choosing whether to chase it... or wait.

What struck me most wasn't just the posture. It was the holes —two small, oval notches carved into its back just behind the shoulders. I stepped in slowly, crouched a bit to get a better look.

"What are these?" I asked gently, pointing to the openings.

Catalina didn't answer right away. She stepped around the table and joined me in the shadowed corner, her expression unreadable.

"They're for wings," she said softly. "A jaguar with wings represents transformation in our culture. Not just strength or survival. But... change. Rebirth."

Her hand drifted—again, almost unconsciously—to rest against her waist. A fleeting touch. So subtle it might have meant nothing. It didn't feel like nothing.

I looked back at the carving. At the soft grooves where wings would eventually emerge. The jaguar wasn't angry or wild. It was poised. Watchful. Waiting.

"And the spiral?" I asked, my gaze tracing along the unfinished curve in the tail. It wasn't the Navarro family's exact mark—it had movement, yes, but with an openness the others didn't have.

"I thought," Catalina said slowly, "that if I could reproduce the old carving, faithful to the original design, he would see we are not broken forever."

She glanced sideways, not at me, but somewhere else entirely—across years, probably. Across memories.

"That we could bridge the gap. Between what was," she said, "and what's still possible."

Her voice softened further.

"Between what's past... and what could still become."

She let her fingers brush the jaguar's flank, then dropped them like she'd held it too long.

"And maybe," she added, "if he saw it that way... maybe this family could mend."

Mozart let out a low exhale, sitting neatly beside the jaguar like he understood it needed guarding.

I didn't say anything. Because I couldn't.

Some things weren't meant to be fixed. Some were meant to be reborn.

I stayed crouched by the jaguar for a long moment after Catalina stepped back. The quiet between us wasn't awkward—it was just heavy, like the kind of silence that settles over things still smoldering long after the fire's out.

I stood slowly, brushing a bit of sawdust from my knee. Mozart gave the jaguar one last reverent sniff and flopped down like a guardian satisfied with his watch.

"You said," I began gently, "that your father wouldn't approve of you carving jaguars again."

Catalina didn't answer right away. The way her shoulders tightened was its own reply.

"Because of your sister?" I added, even softer.

Her eyes darted toward me—sharp—not surprised. She didn't ask how I knew. I don't think she needed to.

"The fire," I said. "People talk. It always comes back to the workshop."

She drew in a long breath and exhaled slowly, like it was something she'd held for years.

"It was late," she said. "Lucía worked at night a lot. She said the jaguar came out clearer after dark—like it waited for everyone else to sleep before it showed itself."

The name clung to the air between us, smoke-thin and breakable.

"No one knows exactly how it started. The wiring was old. There were candles. Paints. Solvents. All of it." Her voice dropped lower. "They say it moved fast. Too fast."

I didn't speak.

"My father—" she stopped, swallowed. "He tried to reach her. They said he went in twice. Came out the second time carrying..." she paused again. "Carrying something. What was left."

Her eyes were far away now.

"They never confirmed anything. Not really. But we knew."

I stayed still. The muscles in my back ached from how hard I was trying not to push.

"His hands were burned so badly the doctors weren't sure he'd keep them. And after that..."

Her voice trailed off. She gestured vaguely at the space around her stall, her work, her stillness.

"That was the end of everything."

I was quiet for a moment, then asked, "You don't think it was just an accident, do you?"

She didn't answer. Not with words. Her eyes said something else. They shifted—toward the jaguar. Toward the holes where wings were meant to go. Then back to me.

"I think grief is a fire too," she said. "And some people never stop feeding it."

I was still watching Catalina, still turning her words over in my head—grief like fire, family like kindling, a jaguar with wings trying to rise from the ashes—when I heard a faint, unmistakable sound.

Gnawing.

Not dramatic chewing. Just a gentle, guilty little scrape-scrape-scrape of teeth on wood. Mozart!

I whirled.

And there he was—my fluffy, cinnamon-churro-scented co-conspirator—curled beneath the edge of Catalina's table, one paw pinning down what appeared to be a very startled-looking frog carving, and his mouth working enthusiastically along its hind leg like it was a chew toy made of dreams and forbidden artisan wood.

"Oh no."

Catalina bent forward just as I reached down.

"Mozart!"

He paused mid-crunch and looked up at me, wide-eyed, tongue slipping out like he was about to ask if I wanted to try a bite too.

"I am so sorry," I said, scooping him up and prying the poor amphibian from his jaws. It was only lightly gnawed—no major damage, just a bit of artistic exfoliation along one thigh. Still..

Catalina looked at the frog. Then at Mozart. Then at me. To her credit, she didn't scream. She just let out the softest sigh I've ever heard land like a curse.

I reached for my wallet. "I insist on paying for it. And I will keep it somewhere far from molars and moral ambiguity."

She gave me a long look, then nodded toward the frog. "He has good taste. That's one of my favorites. It's lucky, too."

"More for you than me," I groaned.

I handed her a few folded pesos, tucked Mozzie under my

arm like a purse with behavioral issues, and gave her a sheepish smile.

"At least he's consistent," Lizzie quipped. "He only chews on things with soul."

I agreed. At that moment, the thought running through my head was it was about time to see what was chewing on Don Abel's soul.

LA COMIDA Y LA CAUSA (THE MEAL AND THE MOTIVE)

Siesta in Oaxaca wasn't a nap. It was a ritual. A hush that drifted into the city like incense through an open window—gentle, insistent, and absolute.

Shops shuttered. Street music paused. Even the dogs seemed to sleep with more purpose.

It was as if the entire city had exhaled at once, folding itself around the scent of simmering beans and the sound of someone's *abuela* flipping tortillas by feel. *Comida* wasn't just the main meal—it was the heart of the day, and everything else adjusted its rhythm to let it beat.

In the streets, shadows stretched longer. Voices softened. There were no loud phones, no rush to be somewhere. Just stillness. Something more deliberate than just silence. I'd spent years in cities that never slept. Oaxaca reminded me what it meant to rest on purpose. We would talk to Don Abel after siesta. Now, it was time to eat.

By the time we reached the painted gate of *Casa de las Bugambilias,* the sun had mellowed to a warm gold and the air was thick with the kind of smell that could derail a to-do list. Cinnamon. Roasted chiles. Garlic. A whisper of chocolate. Something was being stirred in a pot that knew secrets.

The city had gone quiet—siesta hour in full swing—but the kitchen was very much awake.

Mozart trotted ahead, tail high, nose twitching like he was working through a spice matrix only dogs and ghosts could decipher. Lizzie paused at the gate, closed her eyes dramatically, and inhaled like she'd stumbled into a five-star spa where the treatments were edible.

"Is that *mole*? Tell me that's *mole*," she muttered.

My stomach growled—loud enough for Mozart to glance back at me, slightly horrified.

The courtyard buzzed with low voices and the clink of ceramic dishes. Marigolds spilled over the tiled planters, and the hummingbird mosaic on the entry wall shimmered like it was in mid-flight. Everything here felt curated but effortless, as if hospitality were woven directly into the air.

"I think I'm hallucinating tortillas," Lizzie added, clutching her bag dramatically. "Tell me they serve guests."

"They serve," I said, nudging her toward the doorway as Mozart nosed it open for us like a maître d'. "The question is: will you survive it?"

"Only if I go out chewing."

We stepped inside, and the smell hit harder—masa and smoke —and suddenly, murder felt very far away.

At least for now.

The table was already set when we stepped through the archway—handwoven linens dyed in shades of *cochineal,* that deep carmine, and indigo, clay dishes glazed in deep earth tones, and a terracotta vase of marigolds bursting like little suns in the center. A ceiling fan turned lazily above, just enough to keep the air moving and the candle flames flirting with the edges of shadow.

A woman in an embroidered apron smiled and gestured

us toward a spot near the open windows. *"La comida está por servirse,"* she said—lunch is about to be served.

"Saints be praised," Lizzie whispered, already unshouldering her bag like she was settling into a lifelong commitment.

Mozart circled the table legs and flopped beside my chair, tail thudding softly. One of the kitchen staff appeared with a small ceramic bowl filled with *arroz blanco*—simple white rice infused with garlic and epazote—and a generous heap of plain shredded chicken. She placed it on a woven mat with the reverence of a formal blessing.

"Para el perrito sabio," she said with a wink. For the wise little dog.

Mozart beamed, sniffed, and immediately buried his face in the bowl like he'd solved the case and earned his reward.

The first thing I noticed was the calm. No rush. No music. No menus. Just the gentle rhythm of conversation in nearby corners and the clatter of real cooking echoing through the back corridor. A pot simmered. A knife hit a board. Somewhere, a tortilla puffed—air and *masa* conspiring into something holy.

Lizzie reached for a *bolillo*—a crusty white roll that looked like a French baguette with less attitude—and split it open to butter with the urgency of a woman rescuing a kitten from a well.

I followed her lead, taking in the scent as the heat released the tang of fermented dough and faint sweetness from the stone-ground flour.

"This isn't a meal," I murmured.

She paused mid-bite. "Hmm?"

"It's a ceremony," I said. "Everything on this table has a soul."

And judging by the way Lizzie was already sopping up a puddle of melted butter, we were both fully converted.

The first course arrived in wide, shallow bowls—terracotta on the outside, glazed obsidian within, the kind that holds heat like a secret.

Sopa de guías, the woman said with a smile. Squash vine soup.

Steam coiled up into the warm afternoon air, and I leaned in, instinctively taking in the profile: soft green, deeply aromatic, flecked with curls of pale zucchini, tufts of squash blossoms, and the rounded edges of *chochoyotes*—small, dumpling-like orbs made of *masa* with a faint thumbprint pressed in the center, as if the cook had blessed each one before dropping it into the pot.

I took the first bite.

Light, vegetal, and impossibly fresh—as if someone had distilled the taste of a sun-drenched garden into a bowl and stirred in a little homesickness for balance. The broth was infused with *epazote* and garlic. Gently, so as not to overpower the tender greens. The zucchini blossoms added an unexpected silken texture, like flower petals that had learned to melt. The *chochoyotes* were pillowy, earthy, and just toothsome enough to ground the rest of the bowl.

"This soup," I said slowly, "is like a bright spot of spring in the middle of fall."

Lizzie slurped loudly. "This soup is what happens when I forget we're here to solve a murder."

She scooped up one of the dumplings and let it slide onto her tongue like she was at a Michelin-starred tasting menu, then grinned with the unshakable joy of someone finding out soup could flirt.

Mozart gave an enthusiastic tail thump under the table, then looked up as if to say ahem and angled toward Lizzie's knee.

She snuck him a corner piece of *bolillo*. "One bite. You're not solving any murders on an empty stomach either."

The courtyard buzzed with soft conversation and the rhythmic clatter of ladles in distant kitchens. The soup did what good first courses should: it didn't just warm—it opened something. In the palate, in the ribs, maybe even in the case. It made room.

And there was a lot we still needed room for.

The bowls were cleared from every table—guests sighing with satisfaction—and with a grace that made it feel choreographed rather than timed, the next course arrived on broad ceramic platters ringed with hand-painted jaguar motifs. A nod from the universe? Maybe. Or just a reminder that nothing around here came without meaning—especially not the food.

Mole negro con guajolote.

Black mole with turkey.

The sauce—if you could even call something that dense, dark, and unapologetically ancestral a sauce—was poured in a velvety sweep across the plate, pooling like ink beneath two thick slices of slow-roasted turkey thigh. The meat pulled apart under my fork with the ease of a secret slipping loose.

I paused before tasting, just to breathe it in.

Smoke. Clove. Toasted chiles. Roasted nuts. Plantain. Chocolate. A low hum of cinnamon and burnt tortilla—ingredients meant to fight and fall in love in the same pot. The kind of depth you don't get from recipe cards. The kind of flavor that carries lineage.

One bite and I was gone.

Bitter, sweet, earthy, heat that whispers then lingers. A flavor you could get lost in, or climb out of if you needed to feel changed. It wasn't just complex. It was consequential.

Lizzie didn't even bother talking. Just gave a reverent "Mmmmmmmm."

Mozart gave a low, hopeful grunt from under the table. A soft *I sense greatness happening*.

I cut a piece of turkey, dredged it in *mole,* and whispered, "This is a paragraph of a dish."

Lizzie licked her fork clean. "This is a confession. In edible form."

We sat back a little, plates only half-cleared, breathing through the warmth and spice like we were trying to work out what this meal was really telling us.

Because here's the thing about mole negro: it doesn't taste like one thing. It tastes like a hundred truths told in the same breath. Some comforting. Some uncomfortable. Some that burn a little. Kind of like this case.

Somewhere behind us, a breeze carried the faint smell of *cempasúchil,* marigolds from the courtyard altar. I took another bite, the taste blooming on my tongue while a quiet weight pressed behind my ribs. Even Lizzie sat quiet for a beat. That alone said everything.

Just as the mole's last ember settled behind my sternum, a fresh clink of glass and ceramic signaled the next offering—drinks.

One glass shimmered a deep ruby-red: *Agua de Jamaica,* tart hibiscus tea steeped until it tasted like summer's last secret. The other was paler, *Horchata con Tuna Roja*—rice milk swirled with bright pink prickly pear juice, soft and sweet and just a little wild.

I took the *Jamaica* first—cold, sharp, refreshing, the palate-cleanser equivalent of getting slapped with a floral glove. Then the *horchata,* all silk and memory and something vaguely reminiscent of the inside of a childhood dream.

Across from me, Lizzie was double-fisting with complete sincerity.

"We needed this," she said between sips. "*Comida* therapy. So. While my blood sugar stabilizes, where are we in Murder Town?"

I leaned back in my chair and looked up at the red bougainvillea canopying the patio like gossip overhead.

"Victim. Curtis Vale. Charming, smug, and neck-deep in the business of profiting off sacred art without paying for it."

Lizzie tilted her *horchata*. "So, not just a jerk—a thief."

"Exactly."

"Catalina?" I continued. "Defensive. Clearly had a history with him. Angry enough that if she didn't kill him, she probably thought about it."

Lizzie narrowed her eyes. "Did you catch the way she kept touching her stomach when she talked about him?"

I blinked. "You saw that?"

"Yup. Twice. Real gentle. Like something hurt there." She sipped. "You think she's…?"

"I didn't," I said, narrowing my eyes. "But now I kinda do. And if she is…" I trailed off, glancing toward the little blue bowl Mozart had finally licked clean. "Then Don Abel's fury at Curtis wasn't about sketches. It was personal."

Lizzie leaned back and folded her arms like she'd just solved the stock market.

"Think about it. Your daughter gets taken in by a slick foreign art dealer. He steals her designs, maybe ruins her reputation, and then—boom—he leaves her with a baby and no name on the altar. You're Don Abel? You've already buried one daughter. You don't plan to bury another."

I took a sip of jamaica, letting the sour-berry sharpness settle.

"And you sure as hell don't let the man who hurt her walk away smiling."

Mozart let out a low grumble that sounded suspiciously like agreement.

My food critic's brain wanted to move on. My sleuth brain circled back.

A daughter aggrieved. A man silenced. A jaguar with wings.

We were seeing it wrong. Maybe not the story itself—just whose story it was.

"There are still other players on the board, though. Gerardo? Knows more than he's saying. That much is clear. And Molina… same business as Vale, just cleaner about it." I pursed my lips. "It would be really easy to shove someone backward with that cane of his."

"That *red* cane," Lizzie commented.

My eyes widened. "Mozzie's splinter!"

Lizzie's head bobbled. "We may want to get a closer look at that soon."

I nodded in agreement. "Probably a good idea."

"And Soledad?" Lizzie asked.

I hesitated, swirling my jamaica. "She's interesting. She speaks about justice like it's personal. I think Vale didn't just offend her. I think he humiliated her. Maybe made her look the other way when she shouldn't have."

Lizzie finished her horchata with a slurp. "I like her. But she definitely has 'intentionally shoved a man onto the impaling claw of a giant jaguar' energy."

Mozart huffed under the table like he agreed.

I reached for another sip, letting the tart hibiscus linger on my tongue. We'd eaten our way through layers of history and bitterness. And the case felt… similar.

Too many flavors.

Not all of them are evenly balanced.

Dessert arrived without fanfare—just a small, square dish of nicuatole, cool to the touch and dusted with a whisper of cinnamon.

I dipped my spoon into the center and watched the gentle tremble of the custard—more delicate than flan, less assertive than pudding. It looked humble. Unassuming. Like it had nothing to prove.

Then I tasted it.

Corn. Cinnamon. Sugar. Silk. The corn wasn't masked. It was honored. The texture was tender and slightly grainy—just enough to remind you where it came from. It tasted like memory—like something your grandmother would feed you after a bad dream, but only if you asked nicely and promised to be brave.

I didn't say anything for a moment.

Lizzie did.

"Oh my god," she whispered. "If pudding and peace had a baby…"

I nodded. "And baptized it in cinnamon."

Mozart snuffled around the base of the table, then curled up again with a satisfied grunt. His work here was done.

The courtyard had grown quieter. The breeze, gentler. Even the shadows seemed to settle in with full bellies and fewer questions. Mine were still rattling around. The jaguar carving. The spiral on Catalina's piece. The map of grief etched into Don Abel's hands. And now… this new possibility that the motive wasn't just legacy—it was blood.

"So, where does that leave us?" Lizzie asked softly, eyes still on her spoon. "With a dead man who got what was coming… or a dead man who had no idea what he'd set on fire?"

I didn't answer.

Because maybe it was both.

And maybe—like the nicuatole—what mattered wasn't

how it looked on the outside. It what was quietly trembling just beneath.

The table had mostly cleared when a small glass appeared beside my plate—crema de mezcal, milky-white and faintly sweet, served in a clay copita the size of a thimble.

I swirled it once, let the scent bloom: smoke, vanilla, faint citrus, and something older—woodsmoke memory, the ghost of agave long fermented and twice forgiven.

Lizzie raised her own and clinked it gently against mine. "To food as therapy and murder as seasoning."

"May we never reverse the order," I said, and took the tiniest sip.

It was velvety, with a slow-building heat that caught at the back of my throat—not enough to hurt, just enough to remind me I wasn't done thinking yet.

Because I wasn't.

The meal had soothed. The mezcal had warmed. Some flavors don't settle, though. Not right away. Sometimes the truth needed to be served first.

THE MAN AND THE MUSTACHE

The siesta was over and the *mercado* was stretching back to life—shutters lifting, incense reigniting, and the soft thrum of haggling restarting like someone had just hit play.

"I cannot throw shade on any cultural concept that gives me an excuse to have a *cafe con lèche* twice in a single day," Lizzie declared as she sucked down her sweetened coffee.

"Go easy on that stuff. It's a lot stronger than the kind we drink at home." I grimaced. If there was one thing worse than a snack-bingeing Schnoodle, it was an over-caffeinated Lizzie.

She set the coffee on a crumbling retaining wall and started snapping a bazillion pictures. At the rate she was going, we'd have enough photos for an entire book—not just an article.

Ah, well. Whatever puts fuel in the tank, right?

For me, it was answers, and the one person that could give them to me right now was Don Abel.

Shadows pulled back from the walls. The scent of roasted corn and lime peel hung low in the air. Vendors lifted tarps, and children darted past with melting *paletas*. Somewhere nearby, we could hear the occasional crackle of a speaker warming up for whatever celebration was being stitched together next. Everything about the scene said "normal." Normal hour. Normal errands. Normal chaos.

Something was off.

It wasn't anything obvious. No one bumped too close. No one shouting our names across the plaza. Just a faint wrongness that settled in the hollow just below my collarbone. The kind of quiet tension you only notice when you've experienced it before—when you've been watched before. Followed.

Mozart slowed, then glanced over his shoulder—not stopping, not panicking, just tracking. Beside me, Lizzie was already talking about tamarind syrup and whether or not you could sneak back a jar in your carry-on without declaring it as cultural contraband. I let her ramble while I casually adjusted my sunglasses, catching the reflection in a shop window across the lane.

There was a shape. Loose-limbed, tall, moving with just enough intent to raise the hairs on the back of my neck. He wasn't walking toward us. He wasn't even close. But he was there. And he was staying there.

We kept walking.

And so did he.

He didn't trip any wires. He didn't loom or lag or lean into the shadows like a cheap noir extra. He just moved. Carefully. Calmly. The kind of calm that takes effort.

I stopped to pretend I was retightening Mozart's harness, even though it hadn't budged since breakfast. Behind us, I heard footsteps falter. Not dramatically—just a slight syncopation. An offbeat.

The man paused at a tamarind cart. Picked one up. Put it back down. Shifted behind a stack of dried mango and didn't emerge right away. He was trying to blend. Trying to look casual. And if I hadn't already felt him watching, I might've believed him.

The mustache made it an entirely different story.

It wasn't fake—at least not in the costume sense. It was real. Well-trimmed. Too precise. Too self-aware. Like it had been grown for a reason and hadn't gotten the part it auditioned for.

I didn't say anything to Lizzie. She was still three paces ahead, fully locked onto a stall that appeared to sell only marigold crowns and ceramic frogs. Mozart, however, had taken a turn at suspicion. His ears were half-back, his tail stiff in that very specific "I don't like it, but I don't hate it enough to bark yet" kind of way.

Whoever this man was, he was stealthy. Conscious. Calculated. I snorted. I'd been followed in cities less forgiving than this one, and if he thought a clean mustache and a neutral posture were enough to fool me, he clearly had no idea who he was dealing with.

We'd just passed a man selling grilled elotes when I felt him again—closer now. Not menacing, just... steady. Purposeful. Whoever he was, he was watching me like someone who knew what I looked like when I wasn't looking.

I turned.

The man had paused beneath a strand of *papel picado*, feigning interest in a rack of hats he clearly had no intention of purchasing. He turned just enough to keep us in his peripheral vision and not enough to be obvious. It would've been smooth if I didn't have experience with this sort of thing.

And if he didn't have the most recognizable jawline in two hemispheres.

I turned on my heel and started toward him. He pretended not to see me until I was five feet away.

"Nice facial hair," I said. "You look like Hercule Poirot's out-of-work cousin."

The man—Marcus Evans, Interpol liaison, former classmate, and current thorn in my curiosity—sighed through his nose.

"When did you spot me?"

"Almost as soon as you started following us."

If I was being honest, I didn't mind that Marcus was following me one little bit. We had rekindled our university friendship when I managed to get myself tangled in a twisty case back in Ireland. Marcus was a member of the Garda, the Irish police force back then. He'd since moved on, starting a job with Interpol and a long-distance, slow-burn romance with me.

He looked sheepish. "Technically, I was following *you*. Mozart and Lizzie just came with the package."

Beside me, Lizzie made a soft sound of triumph. "Knew it."

He gave her a slight nod—friendly, but distracted. His eyes were still on me.

"I didn't mean to alarm you," he said.

"You didn't. You also didn't call. Or knock. Or use a door like a normal person."

"You don't exactly keep a home address."

Touché.

Mozart trotted forward, gave Marcus a full sniff assessment, and then—apparently satisfied—stood beside him like a tiny, mustachioed endorsement.

Lizzie folded her arms. "So, are we getting the 'just visiting' story, or the real one?"

"What makes you think I'm not just on vacation?" Marcus looked at her, then at me. His jaw twitched once.

Lizzie pointed. "The caterpillar on your upper lip."

"I'm here for work," he admitted.

I stared at him. "But?"

He hesitated.

"But when I saw your name on the hotel registry, I knew you'd already stepped in something."

I didn't answer. I didn't have to.

Because I already knew he was right.

We didn't say much at first. Just walked.

Marcus fell into step beside me like it was instinct. Like we hadn't spent the last few months not texting each other. His stride was steady, his shirt a little wrinkled, his mustache… still clinging to relevance.

"I can't believe you committed to that thing," I said, nodding at it.

He didn't look over. "You noticed it."

"That was kind of the problem."

Ahead of us, Lizzie took Mozart's leash and veered toward a stall selling tamarind-rimmed popsicles shaped like skulls. She gave me a wink, which in Lizzie-speak meant: I'm giving you space, don't waste it.

We slipped past a shaded alleyway that smelled of roasted plantains and wet stone. A breeze stirred the edge of a tattered papel picado banner and lifted the corner of Marcus's sleeve.

"I didn't come here to shadow you," he said finally. "I came because we're tracking something serious."

I arched an eyebrow. "And I'm just conveniently standing in the middle of it?"

"You're rarely just standing."

Fair enough.

We walked a few more steps. The din of the mercado dimmed behind us, replaced by the low thrum of a radio playing boleros from a second-story window. I could feel him watching me in that quiet way he had—never pressing, just… waiting.

"Do they know you're here?" I asked.

"Not yet."

"You've gone off the reservation?"

"More like I'm ahead of the paperwork."

I let that settle between us.

He didn't push. He never did. And that was part of the problem.

Because when Marcus Evans walked beside you, you remembered every time he hadn't.

Still, I didn't stop him. Not when he matched my pace. Not when Mozzie looked back and gave him a soft, approving whuff. Not even when the air between us felt like it was holding its breath.

We passed a row of closed doors painted every shade of Oaxacan sunset—burnt orange, indigo, crimson—and ducked into a quieter side street where even the city's heartbeat felt like it took a breath.

Marcus didn't rush. He never did. I could feel the shape of the words forming in the way his jaw set, the slight flex of his fingers in his pocket.

"I wasn't supposed to be here," he said finally.

"Yet, here you are," I replied. "With a mustache. Bold choices all around."

He gave me a look, half amusement, half fatigue. "Curtis Vale was on our radar."

That stopped me. I turned toward him.

"Excuse me?"

He nodded. "We've had eyes on him for over a year—suspected involvement in a trafficking ring dealing in counterfeit folk art and illegally obtained cultural artifacts. Mostly from Latin America, some from West Africa. High-end buyers. Ugly market."

"Ugly," I repeated, the word sharp in my mouth. "So this wasn't just about stealing sketches and reselling knockoffs?"

"No. That was the bait. The real business was in laundering—smuggling authentic works out under the guise of reproductions, then forging paperwork on the backend. People think they're buying 'inspired by' pieces. They're not."

"And Interpol just happened to send you down here now?"

He exhaled slowly. "We knew he'd be at the festival. What we didn't know was that someone else knew too—and got to him first."

A breeze stirred overhead, setting a tin wind chime jangling behind us.

"And you thought," I said slowly, "that because I was in Oaxaca, I'd... what? Get in the way?"

"No." He looked at me fully then, that unreadable steady gaze that always made me feel like I was missing something important. "I thought you'd be in the middle of it. Because you always are."

I wasn't sure if that was admiration, accusation, or something else entirely.

Maybe he wasn't sure either.

We'd reached the edge of the artisan quarter again—close enough to hear the low thrum of post-siesta shoppers, the occasional bark of a street dog, the clatter of wooden crates being restacked by a vendor with a cigarette tucked behind one ear.

Marcus didn't push. He never had to. Because my brain had already started pulling thread.

Curtis Vale. Trafficking. Forged provenance. Cultural theft with a boutique label. It tracked—too well.

That camera wasn't just for cataloging inspiration. He'd been mapping. Documenting what could be lifted.

"Darcy?" Marcus asked.

I looked up.

"What if he wasn't just stealing from the living?" I said. "What if he was resurrecting something that was supposed to stay buried?"

He frowned. "Explain."

I shook my head. "Not yet. I'm not there. The lines are blurring—past and present. What's lost and what's being taken. Since I've been here, something's been popping up. Something that shouldn't be."

"Tell me more," he murmured.

"Oaxacan art… the *alibrijes*? They're distinct. Each family has a signature style."

"And?"

"And there's one style which isn't, or shouldn't be available anymore. The Navarro style… it seems to be popping up. Not a lot. Just enough." I chewed my bottom lip. "If there's a real market for this type of thing, what would the price be on a rare piece? A style the market *wasn't* flooded with?"

My mind drifted back to the empty display case at the museum. The plaque.

Pieza robada, en proceso de recuperación.

Stolen piece. In process of recovery.

He mentally stayed in step with me. "The price you could command would be… astronomical." His brow furrowed. "But you just finished saying the style isn't available anymore."

I rubbed my chin. "I'm beginning to think someone put it back on the market."

Mozart gave a low, thoughtful grumble. Or maybe that was his stomach.

Still, it felt like a confirmation.

Something had been unearthed. And Curtis Vale had paid for it—not in profit, but in blood.

"Can you use your contacts and check something for me?" I asked.

Marcus's brow creased. "Like what?"

"Something went missing. From the Museo de las Culturas. Can you see if it was reported?"

He stared at me. "You think Vale stole it?"

"Or was working with someone who did."

"And now Vale's dead. You think the piece was a Navarro?"

I thought about the vivid jaguar figurine with the tell-tale swirl I'd seen in the *mercado*.

"Possibly. Which means the piece could still be out there. And if someone's hiding it—someone local—they're either scared… or planning to sell."

He didn't say you're getting too close. It hung there in the space between us anyway. He reached out a hand and brushed a lock of hair from my eyes. I felt the heat flush my chest.

"You think I'm about to trip over it?" I whispered.

"I think if anyone's already halfway to the truth without realizing it—it's you."

I folded my arms. "You could've told me this sooner."

"I could've. Or I could've hoped—for once—that you weren't involved."

He said it without heat. Something, however, sizzled under the surface. It wasn't frustration or duty. It was worry.

"I'll be careful."

Marcus didn't smile. "Good. Just don't be clever when you need to be safe."

I smiled at him as I leaned into him, pressing my hands against his chest. "Now, when have I ever done that?"

In the distance, I could hear Lizzie whispering. "England, Ireland, Scotland, Paris, Bavaria, China, Japan…"

SPLINTERS IN THE DUST

We found her in the shade.

A cluster of pop-up tents had sprung along the south edge of the plaza like mushrooms after a storm—colorful canopies, low benches, and small folding tables that buckled under bowls of carving scraps and dull-edged chisels. One banner read *"Jóvenes Artesanos,"* young artisans, in shaky, hand-painted lettering, flanked by jaguars wearing sunglasses.

María was seated in the center, surrounded by children and splinters. She had her sleeves rolled up and a strip of sandpaper curled between her fingers, helping a boy even out the lopsided snout of what might've once been a coyote. Her hair was pulled back. Her brow furrowed. That wasn't what caught my attention. It was her hands… her hands were graceful. Fluid. Too practiced.

Mozart sat beside me, unusually still. No sniffing. No soft growls. Just alert.

"You see that?" I whispered, watching the way María tilted the carving just so to catch the light. "That's not casual."

We stepped closer.

María looked up and smiled, as if she'd only just noticed us. "*Buenos días*," she said. "We're making spirit animals today. Mostly foxes. Some snails. One terrifying duck… I think."

"Impressive work." I crouched down to Mozart's level and pretended to admire a turtle that had lost most of its limbs. "You're good with them."

"The children, or the animals?"

"In my experience, sometimes it's hard to tell the difference," Lizzie snorted.

"True. Anyway, I'm just helping. I haven't carved in years," she replied lightly, brushing sawdust from her lap. "I only remember a few things from when I was young."

She said it smoothly. Too smoothly.

She passed a chisel to a girl with pink braids and guided her tiny hands through the first curve of a tail. The movement was instinctive—like muscle memory that hadn't been forgotten.

Behind us, the city hummed: children's laughter, street food smoke, a marimba tuning somewhere beyond the next row of stalls.

And then—

A whisper.

Two older women shuffled past the edge of the tent, rosaries in hand, skirts brushing the cobblestones.

"*¿No te parece a la hija de Don Abel?*" one murmured. Doesn't she look like Don Abel's daughter?

"The oldest?" the other replied. "*Sí. La misma barbilla... las manos.* That can't be. That girl died in the fire. They said her body was too far gone. The only thing left was the jaguar, and it was half-burned."

Half-burned? My mind flew back to the jaguar figurine I'd seen in the mercado—the one that made the vendor look like she'd seen a ghost. That jaguar had been crisply painted. No char marks.

The air thickened. The women moved on. María's chisel stopped.

Only for a second. Just an instant in her rhythm. I saw it. Mozart saw it too. His ears dropped half a notch and he shifted his weight closer to my shin.

María stood.

"Excuse me," she said, folding the chisel in a cloth. "I promised to help with the *comparsas* preparation."

"*Comparsas*?" Lizzie questioned.

"The costume parade. It is happening tonight. You should come."

She smiled—gentle, casual, perfect—and walked away. Not hurried. Not awkward. Just... gone.

"Okay," Lizzie said after a beat. "That was weird."

"Did you hear what those women said?"

"Not all of it. Something about a daughter and a fire?"

I stood slowly, brushing off the back of my jeans. My gaze was still locked on the path where María had vanished.

"They said she looked like Don Abel's eldest."

"Wait... the eldest?" Lizzie said. "You mean... the one that—"

"Died," I finished for her. "In the workshop fire. With the jaguar."

Lizzie blinked. "Okay but..." Lizzie looked in the direction María had gone. She blinked twice. "Nooooo," she finally drawled.

"Maybe."

We walked. Quiet now. Not even Mozart clacked his nails. The music and laughter faded behind us, replaced by the hush of hanging vines and the low whisper of dried leaves underfoot.

We turned a corner and found a wall—old, scorched, and crumbling at the edges. The vines hadn't covered it all. I ran my fingers along the charred plaster, the stone beneath brittle and dark.

Fire scars differently. It doesn't fade like paint or wash like blood. It stays.

"If she heard them, she didn't contradict them."

"She also didn't admit anything," Lizzie countered.

"She didn't have to." I closed my eyes for a second. "The way she moved. The way she held the blade. That wasn't learning. That was remembering."

"So, you think she's..."

"I think she's someone worth watching."

Mozart whined gently and pressed against my shin. Not anxious. Just present. Mozzie always knew when something heavy landed in my gut.

I looked down at him.

"She said she hadn't carved in years."

Mozart sneezed on cue.

Lizzie shook her head. "I knew it. You've infected him with your skepticism."

"He's a realist," I said. "With allergies."

We rounded another corner—toward color, toward sound, toward stalls that buzzed with festival energy. The silence stayed with me through it all.

If María was just a volunteer, she was a very skilled one.

If she was more than that—if the whispers were right—then someone who'd been declared dead had been reborn.

We strolled past a wall strung with marigold garlands and shimmering votives, Mozzie trotting quietly between us like he was processing his own theory.

"Okay," Lizzie said, adjusting the tote sliding off her shoulder, "Let's say she is Lucia. Navarro's daughter. The now not-dead one."

"Let's say," I echoed.

"Then why hasn't anyone recognized her?" she asked. "This is Oaxaca. It's not New York. People remember faces here—especially faces attached to workshop fires and family tragedies."

I nodded slowly, watching Mozzie sniff a discarded churro wrapper. "Maybe people don't expect to see what they think is gone. The mind edits. Smooths over the impossible."

Lizzie snorted. "So… town-wide collective memory lapse?"

"Grief does strange things," I said. "And if she vanished young, in trauma, in flames… maybe what people remember is the version of her that existed before. Before the woman she grew into."

Lizzie went quiet for a moment. "I suppose that could be true. Look at me. I look absolutely nothing like my baby picture. My mom swore I was going to grow up looking like Dumbo, but I eventually grew into my ears. See?" She pushed her hair back over her ears which, I had to admit, seemed to be adequately proportioned to the size of her head.

"Her mother's passing," I mused, thinking out loud now. "Maybe she came back because she heard about her mother's passing."

"Do you think Vale knew who she was?" Lizzie continued. "Maybe he was going to expose her?"

"Possibly. He was intimately familiar with the family styles. Maybe he saw her, just like we did, and put two and two together?"

"Maybe," Lizzie mumbled. She drummed her fingers against her leg as we walked. "That still leaves one huge question."

"What's that?"

"Why did she leave in the first place?"

Mozart gave a quiet sneeze and looked up at me like I was only just catching on.

I didn't answer. Because that part—the why—was still burning beneath the surface.

And something told me when it surfaced, it was going to scorch.

THE OLD MASTER'S HANDS

The gate creaked with a disgruntled opinion.

It was beautifully carved—aged cedar, worn smooth around the edges, with a jaguar motif that might have once growled. Now it just looked mildly inconvenienced. Lizzie ran her hand along the top slat and winced when it left a thin trace of rust-colored dust on her palm.

"I'm not saying this place gives haunted vibes," she murmured, "but if a ghost dog shows up wearing an apron and asks for a carving lesson, I'm out."

Mozart sneezed once and trotted forward like he'd been here before in another life. Reincarnated from what, I couldn't guess. Possibly a spice merchant.

The path to the house was overgrown in places—patches of wild marigold and something citrusy that had long since gone rogue. Somewhere under the scents of damp clay and cooked earth was a sharp twist of sun-rotted lime. Not fresh enough to make your mouth water. Just enough to make your nose twitch.

The front porch sagged slightly. The windows were shut against the afternoon heat. A cracked pot full of dried copal resin sat beside the door, its scent faint but unmistakable—like incense at a funeral that ended a few years too late.

Above us, a wind chime clinked—a jaguar claw wrought in tin and strung with glass beads. The beads had faded to ghost-pale, and the claw swayed in a wind that didn't reach the trees.

I raised my hand to knock.

Lizzie stepped back like she was expecting the door to open itself and whisper secrets.

Mozart sat and looked at the door. Then at me. Then back at the door.

"Well," I said quietly. "Let's see if the ghosts are home."

And I knocked.

The door opened just enough to say *not yet*.

Don Abel filled the frame like someone carved by time instead of tools. His presence wasn't imposing, exactly—it was older than that. Rooted. Burnt into the woodwork, like smoke that never quite leaves.

He didn't look surprised to see us. He didn't look glad, either.

His left hand rested against the frame—scarred, the fingers drawn in slightly, like they were holding something invisible. The skin there was pale and papery, stretched across memory.

He didn't speak right away. His eyes moved slowly: Mozart first, then me, then Lizzie.

"You came with the girl," he said.

Not a question.

No *buenas tardes*. No *pásenle*. Just a simple, vaguely accusatory fact. I could only assume he was referencing María.

I smiled politely and shrugged. "We've come with worse."

Beside me, Lizzie gave a small, guilty cough—the sound

of someone who had, in fact, once brought a date to a murder scene.

Don Abel didn't laugh.

He just stepped back—barely—enough to let us in. Didn't mean it was enough to make us feel welcome.

"Do not let the dog chew anything," he said.

"Wouldn't dream of it," I said, nudging Mozart inside like he was a guest at an art museum and not a Schnoodle with questionable self-restraint.

We crossed the threshold, the door groaning shut behind us like it wanted to change its mind.

Inside, the air was thick with something older than dust.

And the ghosts were listening.

The house didn't breathe.

It wasn't neglected—not in the way of cobwebs and peeling paint. It was clean. Ordered. Cared for. But not *lived in*. Like someone had taken their life off the shelf and stored it somewhere out of reach, just until the pain stopped echoing.

The walls were whitewashed and bare, except for a single framed photograph near the door—too faded to make out clearly. It looked like three people standing in front of what might've once been a jaguar. The image was slightly crooked. The nail holding it was rusted. No one had fixed it.

To the right, a modest altar stood near the window—candles melted into shallow bowls, a dish of dried orange slices, and a single sugar skull. The marigolds were real, but brittle, like someone had left them out of obligation.

Lizzie lingered beside me, her gaze darting around. "Is it just me, or does it feel like the air's been holding its breath for ten years?"

"Not just you," I whispered.

Mozart padded forward, nose low, tail still. He made a beeline for a canvas-draped workbench near the far wall and sniffed at the edge of the cloth. A sliver of a jaguar paw—half-carved, unfinished—peeked out beneath the folds.

He didn't bark. Just looked back at me.

Near the hearth, something caught my eye: a broken carving knife. It had been laid carefully on the mantel, the handle wrapped in linen, it's red wood peeking from beneath, the blade snapped at the midpoint like someone had forced the end too far into something it couldn't cut. I didn't touch it. I didn't need to.

Whatever had snapped—metal, muscle, or memory—it hadn't been repaired.

We didn't sit until he did.

Don Abel lowered himself into a worn wooden chair near the altar, like he'd done it a thousand times and still hadn't decided if it was a comfort or a punishment. He gestured vaguely at the bench across from him—not so much inviting us to sit as allowing it.

Lizzie hovered for a second, then sank down beside me with the grace of someone trying not to crunch anything sacred.

Mozart curled at my feet, head on paws, watching Don Abel with the quiet vigilance of a dog who understood this wasn't the kind of man you bark at.

I folded my hands in my lap, trying to match the gravity in the room without letting it swallow me.

"We came to ask about Curtis Vale," I said softly. "I noticed you didn't seem too broken up about his," I paused, searching for the right word, "passing."

He didn't react at first. Then, slowly, he looked at me—not sharp, not startled. Just… heavy. Like his bones remembered something his mouth wasn't ready to say.

"He smiled too easily," Don Abel said finally. His voice was dry, smoke-soaked. "Like someone who steals before he asks the price."

Lizzie stiffened beside me. She stayed silent.

"He came to the market with his camera," he continued, eyes unfocused. "Asking questions he already knew the answers to. Touching what he should not have touched."

"Did you argue with him?" I asked.

Silence.

Then—almost imperceptibly—he shifted his gaze to the hearth. To the broken knife. Then back to me. "I do not waste my breath on liars," he finally growled.

That wasn't a denial. It wasn't quite an admission either. It was something. And in Don Abel's house, something was a lot.

I let the silence settle between us like dust—soft. Telling.

"I've seen Catalina's work," I said gently. "She's... persistent."

Don Abel didn't nod. Didn't smile. Just flexed the fingers of his unburned hand, a quiet twitch that seemed more reflex than response.

"She carves," he said. "Because she is stubborn." He said it the way other people say "breathes."

Lizzie shifted beside me, unsure if that was meant to be praise or indictment.

"Did you teach her?" I asked.

"No." The word was flat. Final. "There is no more carving in the *Casa de Navarro*. Catalina learned what she could by watching when she was younger. What I did not give, she took. What she took, she made her own."

There was no heat in his voice. No scorn. Just the slow ache of something unspoken. A wound he wasn't finished guarding. "Not everyone is born to carry the jaguar," he added.

Mozart let out a small whuff, his head lifting as if he felt the weight in the room shift.

Lizzie leaned forward slightly. "Does the jaguar mean something special? To your family, I mean."

Don Abel didn't answer right away. Then, in a voice low enough I almost missed it: "It was our guardian. Our guide. Passed from hand to hand. Until the fire."

The way he said it—*the fire*—wasn't an event. It was an era. And whatever the jaguar had meant before that moment... it had not survived it. At least, not for him.

The word *fire* seemed to linger in the air longer than it should have. Outside, a breeze stirred the wind chime again—soft, metallic, brittle. Inside, nothing moved.

I shifted slightly on the bench. The wood creaked under me, dry from age, like it hadn't carried conversation in a long time. My fingers brushed the hem of my linen blouse, suddenly aware of the heat in the room—not oppressive, but baked in. The kind that sinks into the adobe and never fully leaves.

"I've heard pieces," I said cautiously. "About the workshop. The fire. Your daughter..."

Don Abel's good hand closed into a fist.

Beside me, Lizzie stopped mid-fidget. Mozart lifted his head, alert.

"I'm not here to pry," I added, voice low. "I just... want to understand."

Don Abel stared into the corner, somewhere above the altar. His jaw worked once, twice.

"Some things burn because they are meant to," he said, voice sandpaper rough. "Others burn because someone wants them gone."

He didn't look at me. He didn't have to. The altar's single candle flickered as if it had just heard its own name.

Lizzie gave a weak laugh—too brittle to be funny. She tugged at my sleeve, leaned in, and whispered, "Remember what I said about that ghost?"

Mozart let out a low sound, somewhere between a whine and a hum.

I glanced toward the hearth again. The broken knife. The unfinished jaguar. The silence that hummed around them like a threat no one had dared speak aloud.

Someone had lost more than art in that fire. And not everything that burned had turned to ash.

"I saw a carving," I said after a moment, careful to keep my tone light. "In the mercado. A jaguar with orangey red spiral markings—Navarro style, I think."

That got his attention.

Don Abel's eyes snapped to mine. The flash of disinterest vanished like a match dropped in alcohol.

"*Navarro naranja*. A special pigment and design our family created. It should not be used," he said, his voice low and tight. "Not without blessing. Not without blood."

Not without blessing or blood.

My thoughts tumbled in my head. It certainly didn't seem that Don Abel was giving anyone—not even Catalina, his own daughter—a blessing to carry on the family's carving tradition.

So, had Don Abel exacted the other from Curtis Vale? Blood?

Lizzie blinked. "Well," she murmured, "that's festive."

I didn't smile. Neither did Don Abel. I shifted slightly forward. "The patterns were exact. Even the painted tail swirls."

He didn't respond right away. Something in his posture had changed—no longer guarded, exactly. Just... bracing. "It is a sacred design," he said finally. "Not for tourists. Not for thieves. It was passed down through hands that understood what it meant to carve something from wood—and what it cost."

He didn't have to say the word *Lucía*. It was already in the room. His eyes dropped to his hand—the scarred one, curled like it remembered the heat. "After the fire, I sealed the tools. The style died with my daughter. It is not mine to give anymore."

"Someone's carving it," I said gently.

Don Abel looked past me. Past the room. "Then someone is pretending to carry what was never theirs to hold." He stood slowly, walking to the altar. Adjusted a candle. Didn't meet my gaze.

Outside, wind rustled the trees. Inside, everything went still again. And the jaguar watched from beneath the drop cloth. Waiting.

He stayed facing the altar, his hand steadying the edge of the wooden frame, knuckles white.

I didn't press. I didn't let it drop, either.

"There are rumors," I said carefully, "that Curtis Vale was pressuring people. Taking things he didn't have a right to. Sketches. Patterns. Secrets. Maybe more."

Don Abel's shoulders didn't move. Something in the air around him did—like tension radiating outward in quiet, concentric circles.

"He took what did not belong to him," he said at last.

I waited, heart ticking.

"Not just the pattern," he continued. "Not just the legacy."

He turned then, slowly. The light caught the deep lines in his face, turning them into canyons.

Lizzie swallowed. "You mean—he stole more than art?"

Don Abel didn't answer her. Mozart shifted at my feet, letting out a breath that sounded suspiciously like a warning.

"What exactly did he take?" I asked softly.

Don Abel's mouth opened. Then closed. The words hovered there, unsaid. His jaw worked once. His gaze dropped.

"To take a carving is one thing," he murmured. "To take something that breathes..." He trailed off.

I stared at him. Lizzie did too. There was a pain behind that silence that felt sharper than any knife. And suddenly, I didn't think he was talking about tradition anymore. Or legacy. Or even the fire.

Something had been taken from this man that couldn't be remade. And if it was what I suspected...

Then Curtis Vale hadn't just stolen art. He'd stolen something much more dangerous.

Love. Trust. Blood.

And someone, somewhere, had made him pay for it.

I let the silence hang for a few long seconds.

Don Abel walked back to his chair. He didn't sit. Instead, he reached for a small clay cup on the nearby table and took a slow sip. I caught a faint whiff of *tejate*—fermented maize and cacao—earthy and bitter with a hint of rose. The kind of drink that lingered.

"You think I killed him," he said, eyes level.

"I don't want to think so," I said honestly. "I think you may have had reason to want to."

Lizzie straightened beside me. Mozart, who'd been quietly chewing the corner of a woven doormat, froze.

Oh, boy, I hope Don Abel didn't see *that*. I shot Mozart a scolding look. He dropped the mat and rested his furry chin on his paws.

Don Abel exhaled hard through his nose—half-laugh, half wound. "If I had killed every man who dishonored what I loved, I would have no hands left."

He held up his scarred one.

The light caught the ridges—twisted rope-like burns that curled from wrist to palm. A topography of pain. A map no one would choose to draw.

"I did not kill that man," he said. "If he is dead, it is no tragedy to me."

Mozart whined, ears twitching. My fingers brushed the back of his neck, grounding both of us.

"Then whose tragedy is it?" I asked.

He didn't answer. Instead, he turned his back again—toward the unfinished jaguar, the altar, the quiet echo of something long buried.

He didn't walk us out.

Just turned away like he'd already said everything he meant to, and maybe a few things he hadn't. The door creaked open behind us—not by his hand, but mine—and even that felt like trespassing.

Lizzie stepped outside first, blinking against the late afternoon glare. I paused on the threshold. Looked back. The shadows in the house had deepened. I could still see the curve of the jaguar under its shroud. Still feel the tension coiled in the room like a breath held too long. Mozart gave one last look back too, then padded down the steps without a sound. We crossed the yard in silence, the marigold heads brushing against our calves like they were trying to stop us. Lizzie didn't speak until we were just about to the courtyard exit. "That was... intense."

"Yeah."

"You still think he didn't kill Vale?"

"I think he didn't need to," I answered. "Did you see the expression on his face? Don Abel could bury a man with a look."

Mozart stopped beside the low wall and sniffed at something in the dirt. He pawed the ground. The branches of a plumeria tree hung heavy over the courtyard wall—its last blooms of the season littering the ground. "Mozzie! Leave it."

The last thing I needed was for Mozart to get sick abroad from eating a flower. As I drew closer, I could see that wasn't what he was pawing at at all. Something lay half-buried in the soil. I bent to pick some up.

Lizzie squinted at it. "What is that? Wood shavings? All the way out here?"

I nodded. "Don Abel made it pretty clear, no one has carved at his home in years." I looked up. From this vantage point, I could see Don Abel through an open window. His shoulders shook. It almost looked like he was crying. Then my gaze drifted to the thick branches of the plumeria—branches that would have made it easy for someone to scale the wall, even if the courtyard gate was locked.

Mozart bumped my leg with his nose. I ruffled his fur. "I think someone stood here watching Don Abel."

"And decided to whittle?"

I pushed the shavings around in my palm. Despite what Don Abel had told us, someone was carving. Someone who shouldn't be.

And suddenly, I wasn't sure who the real ghost in this story was.

SPLOTCHES & SKELETONS

We left Don Abel's house in a silence that wasn't quite awkward. It wasn't entirely finished, either.

He hadn't walked us out. He hadn't needed to. The weight of what he'd said—and what he hadn't—was still trailing behind us like a veil of smoke.

By the time we rounded the corner back toward the plaza, the sun was starting to slide down behind the church towers, bleeding gold over the rooftops and turning the air to warm bronze. Mozart trotted a few steps ahead, sniffing every corner like he was taking stock of the city's sins. Lizzie walked beside me, unusually quiet until the first burst of brass split the air like a cork from a shaken bottle.

"Ooh," she said, perking up. "This feels festive. Possibly haunted, but festive."

The comparsas had begun.

The street in front of us swelled with people—locals, tourists, and elaborately dressed performers all converging into one glitter-dusted stampede of color and noise. Someone in full skeletal bride attire twirled past us, her papier-mâché veil catching the wind. A child dressed as a monarch butterfly darted between legs. A costumed jaguar with papier-mâché paws waved at no one in particular.

And through it all, the music roared—brass, drums, whistles, and something that may or may not have been a firework shaped like a rooster.

Mozart barked once, then sneezed theatrically and trotted back to my side, unimpressed.

I narrowed my eyes at the chaos ahead.

"Do you really think now's the best time for a parade?" I muttered.

Lizzie grinned and elbowed me lightly. "You mean the sacred ancestral celebration that predates your travel anxiety? Yeah. I think it's gonna happen with or without us."

She wasn't wrong. The street was a living organism, pulsing with laughter and rhythm. If Don Abel's house was a tomb of unfinished grief, the comparsa was a resurrection. I couldn't stop thinking about the wood shavings, though. About the unfinished jaguar. About the mysterious pattern that kept popping up, and the splinter of red on María's sleeve.

Curtis Vale may have died for stealing something sacred. The deeper question was, who was still carving Navarro style?

And why?

We still needed to talk to Dr. Pineda again, pin down her connection to the museum theft. We needed to find Molina —if he hadn't already slithered back across the border with his knockoff empire.

Mozart let out a quiet whuff and nudged my calf, just as a towering papier-mâché devil with accordion arms lurched past us.

Lizzie clasped her hands. "This is amazing. I need three photos, a video, and I saw this wonderful *huipil*. It's this gorgeously colorful dress with embroidered flowers. I've got to have it.."

"Stay close," I said, pulling her back before a *Maríachi* on stilts could take her out. "This isn't just a parade. It's the perfect place to hide something in plain sight."

Or someone.

Because in a crowd of masks, it's hard to tell who's watching whom.

The deeper we pushed into the comparsa, the more it swallowed us.

The crowd didn't walk so much as it swayed—one collective, costumed tide pulled forward by brass and bass and the scent of roasted corn mixed with fireworks. Papel picado ribbons crisscrossed the street overhead in deep purples, sunburst oranges, and flame reds, flickering like tongues in the breeze. Music thundered out of half a dozen competing sound systems, all clashing and harmonizing in that distinctly Oaxacan way that somehow made it feel like celebration and ceremony were the same thing.

A skeleton couple tangoed past in full formalwear, the woman's dress made entirely of layered black lace and paper flowers. Behind them, a group of schoolchildren dressed as dancing devils launched confetti bombs into the crowd and screamed with glee as adults ducked and laughed. To my left, a man in a glowing skeleton mask spun fire on a tether and nearly caught a balloon vendor's cart on its last swerve.

Lizzie twirled toward me, one of those flower-crown halos now slightly askew on her head and glitter on her cheek. "Can I just say, if I go missing, I want it to be in a parade. Preferably while wearing something with sequins and a metaphysical backstory."

I raised an eyebrow. "So... basically this?"

"Exactly this."

Mozart, thoroughly unimpressed by the fanfare, walked

between us like a bodyguard with seasonal allergies—occasionally sneezing at plumes of smoke and giving side-eye to any costumed performer who got too close. He pulled toward the edges of the street now and again. I kept the leash firm.

Every few steps I scanned the crowd—half looking for clues, half just trying not to lose Lizzie in a cluster of skeletal acrobats.

Because in all the color and chaos, it was easy to forget we were still chasing something.

Or someone.

And whoever it was had left just enough of a trail to feel like an invitation. I just hadn't decided if it was to a dance.

Or a trap.

We'd just made it past a brass ensemble in full skeletal drag when Mozart veered slightly to the left, paused, and lifted his nose like someone had lit a churro-flavored candle just for him.

I followed his line of sight—and froze.

There, across the plaza, half-shadowed by a stall stacked high with papel picado fans and woven bracelets, stood María. She wasn't in costume. She wasn't in character. Just... there.

Same sun-faded denim jacket. Same steady calm that somehow always felt like a whisper you weren't meant to overhear. She stood next to a group of tourists snapping selfies with a fire-spitting devil float, her hands folded neatly in front of her, expression unreadable.

She wasn't shopping. She wasn't gawking. She was observing—with the quiet attentiveness of someone who once belonged here, but hadn't in a long time.

Mozart let out a low puff of air, more curiosity than concern.

I didn't move closer. Just watched.

The devil float rolled past her, and for a moment she was backlit—her jacket catching the light from the marigold garlands strung along the rooftops. That's when I saw it.

A vivid splotch of color high on the shoulder blade—flame-orange, bordering on red, almost too bright for fabric, too fresh to have been from long ago. It matched the jaguar figurine from the mercado almost exactly. Those same violent hues—furious, beautiful, unforgettable.

Lizzie, oblivious, leaned into me. "Please tell me you see the skull made entirely out of churros."

"I see something," I murmured.

It wasn't sweet. It was strange. Because María—who wasn't carving, wasn't painting, wasn't *anything*—was wearing the story on her sleeve. And someone, somewhere, was going to have to explain why.

"Is it me, or does that color look incredibly familiar?" I spoke loudly over the noise.

"Huh?" Lizzie only half paid attention to me as one of the parade marchers swept her up in a festive twirl.

"That color." I pointed toward María across the plaza.

Lizzie laughed as the twirl spun her into me. We almost went down in a pile of arms and legs. "What are you talking about? In a place like this," she gestured as she righted herself then helped me to my feet, "it's a riot of color."

"Not like *that* one. Navarro *naranja*."

She didn't get a chance to answer. A papier-mâché skeleton with a ten-foot wingspan clipped a lamppost and went down like a drunk angel.

The crowd yelped. Brass notes curdled. Someone screamed—not in terror, more in theatrical dismay—and a whole section of the comparsa heaved sideways like a dance line gone rogue.

María vanished.

Not in a puff of smoke or a swirl of villainous laughter—

just *gone,* like she'd stepped between the notes of the song and found the quiet space where no one looked.

I surged forward. A parade marshal in a devil mask stepped into my path, arms wide and panicked. "*¡Cuidado! ¡Cuidado!*" he shouted. "Careful!" He gestured wildly toward the fallen skeleton float now tangled in a streetlamp and what looked like a floral installation shaped like a flamingo.

Mozart barked sharply, pulling against the leash.

I turned a tight circle, scanning the crowd. The party continued. The devil float—further down the street. And María? She could've been anywhere.

"Tell me that wasn't the symbolic collapse of the patriarchy," Lizzie chuckled.

"I lost her," I muttered, still looking.

"Wait—who? María? Is that who you've been yammering on about?" She craned her neck above the crowd like a caffeinated meerkat. "You think she saw us?"

"I think she saw me see her."

Mozart gave a low grumble and circled back toward the alley just behind the papel picado stall. It was already too late. The parade had swallowed her whole.

We regrouped at the churro cart like war generals with a serious sweet tooth.

The cart itself was a wheeled wonder of cinnamon and chaos—its awning sagged a little on one side, but the fryer hissed with promise, and the vendor worked with the rhythmic speed of a man who'd survived six festivals and lost hearing in one ear. Strings of papel picado fluttered above us, dyed gold and magenta, and the air shimmered with grease, sugar, and something almost floral—maybe the tub of hibiscus syrup perched next to a bowl of lime zest.

Mozart plopped down at my feet with a heavy sigh, head on paws, ears twitching at every sizzle.

"Okay," Lizzie started. "Let's back up. You saw María.

Standing still. Looking… what? Suspicious? Angelic? Slightly cultish?"

"Calm," I said. "Too calm. And out of place. Not observing the parade—watching the people."

Lizzie nodded solemnly. "Creepy adjacent."

"And she had paint on her jacket."

That got her attention. "Like *paint* paint?"

"Reddish orange. Same saturated tones from the jaguar figurine in the mercado. Almost the exact same shade."

Lizzie blinked. "So either she bumped into the world's most festive *piñata*, or—"

"She's connected to the carving. Somehow."

We watched the crowd roll past again—dancers, musicians, vendors, a papier-mâché *Xoloitzcuintli*, a Mexican hairless dog, with LED eyes.

I tapped my notebook against my leg. "The Navarro style's not just showing up in stalls anymore. The signature color is showing up on her. On her clothes."

"So, what are we thinking? Art smuggler in disguise? Long-lost carving prodigy with a secret identity?"

I didn't answer. Because somewhere behind the cinnamon sugar and the Maríachi brass, my gut had already made its wager. And Mozart—who had suddenly tilted his head—seemed to agree.

Of course, that could have just been his confusion at the sight of a giant, hairless dog.

THE KISS AND THE CLUE

The comparsa continued winding through the streets. Somewhere behind us, a band blared a rhythm so fast it made my heart feel like it was trying to learn salsa. The scent of roasted corn and lime peel hung thick in the air, undercut with cinnamon, gunpowder, and the ghost of fried dough.

Mozart sneezed. Once. Then again. Then gave me a look that translated to *you people are insane.*

Lizzie had sugar in her eyes.

"I'm taking him to the *mercado* again," she announced, already unhooking Mozart's leash from my wrist like I was just borrowing her dog for a while. "He saw some souvenirs he absolutely must have. He told me so." Mozart tilted his head at her.

I raised a brow. "Is that what we're calling it now?"

She didn't even blink. "He has a marvelous eye for folk art, Darcy. Don't be stingy with the souvenir budget, Darce. We're supporting the local economy."

"And your shopping fix."

"It's the same thing."

She winked and melted into the crowd, Mozart in tow and both of them on a mission. I watched her go, part amused, part deeply suspicious.

The music surged. A float shaped like a flaming skeleton rolled by, its ribcage lit from within. Children in monarch wings squealed and darted through the crowd like butterflies skipping reincarnation altogether.

And me?

I just stood there, the ghosts of everything I'd learned pressing in around me—Don Abel's grief, Curtis's betrayal, Catalina's quiet rebellion, and María's jacket with that too-fresh splash of jaguar-paint orange.

My thoughts were louder than the brass band. And just as out of tune.

I was just watching a skeleton on stilts toss marigolds like confetti grenades when I felt it—that shift in the air. Not the kind that comes with a gust of smoke or a new float. The kind that sets your nerves whispering before your brain catches up.

"Darcy."

My name slipped through the noise, low and sure, barely louder than the thump of the drums. It cut straight through the chaos. I turned.

There he was. No mustache this time. Just Marcus. Back in his usual too-wrinkled-to-be-threatening button-up, his sleeves rolled, his hair wind-mussed and doing nothing to downplay the sleep deprivation clinging to his jawline. He smelled like cedar and airplane soap and someone who hadn't had time to unpack—but was already ten steps ahead.

He fell into step beside me without asking. Like he always did. Like he never stopped.

My shoulder brushed his. Just once. A glancing thing. The heat of it spread a little farther than it should've. I didn't flinch. Neither did he. Neither of us moved away.

I gave him an appreciative once-over., "No mustache. Tragic loss to undercover fashion."

He gave me a sideways glance. "I was wondering if you'd pick up on it."

"Details about you are hard to miss," I murmured, meaning it more than I meant to.

He looked ahead, but the corner of his mouth lifted—just barely. "So, how's my competition?"

I stopped walking and looked at him cross-eyed. "What?"

Marcus chuckled. "You know. Short guy. Kinda furry. Seasonal allergies."

Mozart.

I started walking again, noticing Marcus's gaze occasionally darting toward the crowd. "Well, he's loyal, food-motivated, and snores less than most men I've dated."

"Sounds like a keeper."

We walked on.

The crowd swelled around us—color and smoke and brass. And there, tucked between skeletons and saints, I let myself enjoy the fact that Marcus was beside me. That he was here.

We drifted past a street corner where a papier-mâché skeleton couple slow-danced to a brass rendition of "Besame Mucho." The bride's veil flared every time she spun. The groom's bowtie had seen better centuries.

Marcus didn't see any of it. His eyes were trained on a linen-clothed back walking stiffly through the crowd, leaning on a cane.

Molina.

"How goes the case?" I ventured.

"We're still trying to pin down the supply chain. We always knew Curtis was the charming face. In light of recent events—well, the higher ups now definitely think someone else was pulling the strings."

"A partner?"

"Someone local," Marcus said. "Someone who knew what was hidden… and how to move it."

"Is that why you're following Molina?"

An embarrassed grin broke across Marcus's face. "Of course, you figured that out."

"Didn't have to be a genius. He's in a similar business as Vale. You've had eyes on him since you walked up. And I'd recognize that red cane anywhere."

He nodded once. "Like I said, we suspected, but never had enough on him," he said, voice low. "Too careful. Always let Curtis be the face of things. He's definitely been on the radar."

"You really think they were partners?" I asked.

Marcus glanced sideways, careful not to break pace. "Silent partners. Molina had access, contacts, and credibility in Oaxaca. Curtis had charm, cash, and plausible deniability."

"And now that Curtis is dead…"

"Molina's either scrambling to cover his tracks—or continuing the business on his own terms."

A costumed jaguar brushed past us—papier-mâché head oversized and painted in luminous purples and golds. For a second, it seemed to look straight at me.

"The way Interpol figures it, Molina was the risk manager," Marcus continued. "Curtis could poke the bear because Molina knew which ones wouldn't bite."

"And you think he's gone rogue?"

"I think the mask came off the minute Vale crossed him," he said. "There's a lot of money in unregistered cultural heritage—especially if the piece in question was believed to have been destroyed. You put something like the Navarro jaguar back on the market, you don't just fetch a price. You make headlines."

"And enemies."

He nodded grimly. "Which means someone else might be looking for it too. And not everyone plays by international extradition rules."

The roar of a brass section surged nearby, swallowing the edges of his words. I didn't need volume to hear what he wasn't saying.

He wasn't just following Molina. He was circling the fire, trying to figure out who else was holding the match.

"You could've warned me, you know," I said, eyes forward, voice even.

Marcus didn't answer right away. The air between us shifted—like the pause between thunder and its echo.

We turned down a narrower street, quieter for a few steps. Overhead, papel picado flapped like wings in the rising breeze, casting shadows that danced across his face. He looked younger in this light. Or maybe just more tired.

"I didn't think you'd get this close," he said finally. "You were supposed to be here for food, Darcy. Festivals. Articles. Your usual brilliance—just not this kind of brilliant."

His voice had a tight edge—like regret and admiration had gotten into a wrestling match and neither was winning.

Something in my chest did a slow somersault. Not fear. Not quite pride either. Just the strange weight of being seen too clearly by someone you weren't sure you wanted to hide from.

We walked in step for a few more paces. His hand swung a little wider than before—barely— enough that his fingers brushed mine.

Just the edge. He didn't pull away. Neither did I. Around us, the comparsa roared back to life, swallowing the moment in confetti and brass. I felt it all the same. And I think he did too.

A burst of laughter turned my head.

Under the boughs of a tree whose petals drifted like

confetti from the branches, a young man held out a bundle wrapped in stiff brown paper. The girl beside him—a festival sash slung loose over one shoulder and glitter pressed into the creases of her smile—giggled as she reached for it.

The paper crinkled as she unwrapped it, careful, hesitantly curious, until a bundle of wildflowers spilled out—dyed the bright, impossible colors of the parade: turquoise, coral, violet so bold it nearly glowed. The bouquet was messy and mismatched and utterly perfect. A gift that had no purpose other than joy.

I smiled.

And then my smile faltered. Because it wasn't the flowers that caught me—it was the paper. Not the color. Not the string.

The package.

It was long. Tight. Intentional. Like something meant to stay together until the exact right moment. And as the girl unwrapped it, my brain rewound like a record needle dragging back over the same groove.

The airport. María—standing by the curb, arms full of brown paper and tension. A long, wrapped bundle clutched tight against her chest. Then Curtis. The shove. The cab. The blur of wheels and ego and English. And after that?

No paper. No parcel. Just María with empty arms.

I stared at the young couple a second longer, but I wasn't seeing them anymore. My focus had tunneled into a memory I hadn't realized I'd filed under *unresolved.*

Beside me, Marcus shifted. "What is it?"

I didn't answer right away. Because suddenly I wasn't sure the most important thing Curtis Vale stole... was Catalina's sketches.

I saw Marcus's jaw clench a split second before I followed his gaze.

Gerardo Molina.

He stood directly across the street, flanked by a skeletal puppet and a woman with glitter painted over half her face. His eyes paid them no mind. They were locked on us. Not casual. Not curious. Direct. Pinning.

"Marcus," I whispered.

"I know."

"What do we do?"

"We disappear," he said—just as the music crescendoed and the parade crowd surged again.

And then he kissed me.

Not a soft maybe. Not a polite brush. A cover. A cloak. The kind of kiss that rewrites your posture and repurposes your breath.

One arm slid around my waist, the other braced gently against my neck, tilting me into him like this was muscle memory. Like he'd practiced in dreams and finally stopped waiting for the rehearsal.

At first, I froze—not from shock, but from the realization that we had passed the threshold of pretending.

Because this wasn't just about Gerardo.

This was Paris. Ireland. The late-night phone calls. The almosts we never finished.

My hands landed on his chest. My intent wasn't to push away. I wanted to memorize. The slope of muscle beneath the cotton of his shirt. The steady pound of his heartbeat—too fast, too familiar.

The confetti fell like ash and stars. The air tasted of gunpowder and cinnamon. And for the span of a few long seconds, I wasn't thinking about alebrijes or Navarro spirals or stolen sketches.

Just him. Just us. When we finally pulled apart—slower than either of us probably meant to—I was the one to speak first.

"Well," I said, blinking. "That was... strategic."

Marcus didn't smile. Not quite. "Camouflage," he said.

"Sure," I murmured, still breathless. "Just trying to blend in with all the other emotionally repressed secret agents kissing their college sweethearts on the Day of the Dead."

His hand lingered at my waist a beat longer than necessary. And Gerardo was gone.

I gently stepped back. I took the warm feel of him along with me. I couldn't help the stupid smile on my face. Apparently, neither could he.

Then, my smile evaporated. Marcus stepped toward me alarmed. "What's wrong?"

The crowd surged again, swallowing the space where Gerardo had stood like the street itself was in on the trick. Costumed dancers in papier-mâché antlers leapt through the mist of another firework, and the sky went briefly lavender from the smoke.

I exhaled, pressing a palm to my forehead. I didn't feel faint. My thoughts were just starting to spiral. Not about the kiss. (Okay, maybe *a little* about the kiss.) Mostly it was about the way Marcus had spoken of Molina. Confident. Focused. Perhaps a little too neat.

I turned to him, still tucked in the narrow ribbon of shadow between parade floats. "What if you've got the partner wrong?"

Marcus arched an eyebrow. "Come again?"

"You said Interpol suspected Molina. That he had access, motive, and local knowledge. He fits the profile." I paused.

"What if Molina wasn't the partner?"

Marcus didn't answer right away. A nearby trumpet blared a sour note and Mozart sneezed as he and Lizzie continued winding through the crowd nearby. Somewhere behind us, a skeletal horse clattered on wheels.

He tilted his head. "Go on."

"Rare pieces. Formerly 'lost' pieces." I looked into

Marcus's eyes. " You said those were the ones that commanded the highest prices, right?"

Marcus folded his arms across his broad chest. "Yes. If we're figuring the law of supply and demand. If only one is in supply, the demand—the cost—would likely skyrocket."

"But Vale wasn't making money just *hoping* those kinds of pieces would fall out of the sky."

"Seems unlikely."

"So, hear me out. Molina might be a slippery fish, but he's not a carver. Someone had to do the hands-on work. Someone who knew the style. Who could replicate a piece convincingly enough to fool the buyers, maybe even Don Abel himself."

I glanced down at my fingers, absently curling them into a fist. "What if *someone else* was the source—and Vale cut *them* out?"

Marcus studied me, his expression unreadable. "You think Molina wasn't the partner?"

I shrugged. "I think we've been following the flash. I think the fire might've started somewhere quieter."

He nodded once, slowly.

"Then who," he asked, "do you think lit the match?"

The fireworks had faded into a low throb against the sky. My thoughts sharpened. We passed a vendor selling glowing skull balloons, and I didn't even blink at the neon.

"Marcus," I said slowly, "you asked who Vale's partner might have been."

He glanced over, eyes narrowed. "You have someone in mind?"

"Maybe." I watched a lone firework soar and fizzle. "That first day—when Lizzie and I landed—I met a woman. Said her name was María. She looked like she'd just gotten off a flight, too. Now… I'm not so sure."

"Go on," he said.

"She was holding this long, paper-wrapped parcel. No luggage. No backpack. Just this... package. She appeared nervous. Like she was waiting for someone. Then Vale shoved past her, stole her cab—and that package disappeared with him."

Marcus stopped just long enough to let a sugar skull float pass before he replied. "You think she wasn't arriving. You think she was meeting him."

"I think it's possible. That she was meant to hand something off. I think he took it before the deal happened. Changed the rules on her."

"And she's been circling ever since—trying to fix it."

"Or cover her tracks. Or maybe both."

He nodded once.

"Maybe that's what triggered everything." I hesitated. "Maybe she was the partner Interpol's been chasing all along."

Lizzie reappeared like a mirage conjured by cinnamon and mischief, a half-eaten churro in one hand and powdered sugar streaked through her bangs like she'd been in a festive baking accident. Mozart trotted proudly beside her, licking his chops and radiating the smug satisfaction of a dog who had absolutely broken the no-snacks rule.

"Something tells me you," Lizzie began, arching a brow as she sized us up, "got into something a heck of a lot sweeter than a churro."

Marcus glanced away, feigning interest in a passing marigold cart. I opened my mouth. Closed it again. Because there wasn't a single answer I could give that wouldn't confirm something I wasn't ready to name.

Lizzie narrowed her eyes. "Huh."

She took another bite of churro, chewed thoughtfully, and leaned in like she was about to comment further—until she caught the look on my face.

Not at her. Not at Marcus. Downward. Inward.

I was staring at the dust on the street. Or maybe not the dust. Maybe the trail of memory curling up from the edge of something sharp and dangerous that had only just begun to take shape. There was no firm theory, not yet. Motive, on the other hand?

Oh, I was staring right at it.

And it was beginning to look a lot like betrayal wrapped in brown paper.

Mozart sneezed once and sat beside me, like a sentinel on a sugar high. Lizzie handed me the rest of her churro without a word.

I didn't eat it.

I was already full—with firelight, fresh suspicion, and the feeling that something sacred had been taken, and someone wasn't done paying for it.

SACRED AND STOLEN

The *Museo de las Culturas* was quieter in the morning light—less holy, more hollow. Unlike my brain which was chockablock with tumbling thoughts about last night's kiss with Marcus, the possibilities we'd discussed about the case, and stolen *alibrijes*.

The tourists hadn't yet swarmed, and the sunlight through the high windows painted the ancient stone floors in neat geometric shapes, like the building was trying to be orderly.

I slipped past a trio of volunteers straightening up an ofrenda display and followed the familiar hallway to the folk art archive tucked near the back. Lizzie and Mozart had stayed behind, reluctant to stir.

A few of the rooms smelled like varnish. This one smelled like paper, dust, and the stubborn kind of silence that only ever means someone's hiding something. Soledad stood by a set of rolling shelves, reshelving photo folios with the deliberate care of someone who was used to handling both treasures and time bombs. Her blouse today was black with thin red piping, the collar starched just enough to suggest she wasn't thrilled to see me again.

"Good morning," I offered lightly.

She turned, gave a faint nod. "Señorita Finnegan."

Technically accurate. Ominously formal.

"I wanted to thank you," I said, feigning breezy. "The insight you gave us about the Navarro family the other day... It's helped me understand so much more about the context surrounding their work. And the tragedy."

Soledad slid the last folio into place, her fingers pausing on the edge as if measuring how much patience she had left.

"The comparsa was beautiful last night," I added. "Powerful, really. You could feel the history walking alongside you."

That got her attention. She turned, lips pursed. "History is always walking alongside us, Miss Finnegan. Some people are just better at pretending not to see it."

"Some people," I agreed, "prefer to take it and sell it."

She blinked once. That was all. It made things pretty clear, though. We weren't dancing anymore. We were squaring off.

I paused in front of the empty display case—the same one I'd noticed on our last visit. Still unfilled. Still glaringly obvious in a room otherwise curated down to the tilt of each label.

"Still no replacement?" I asked, nodding toward the plaque: *Yaguar enmascarado. Robado.* Winged jaguar figure. Stolen.

Dr. Pineda didn't look up from the stack of accession forms in her hands. "There won't be."

I raised an eyebrow. "You're keeping an empty case on display?"

"It's not empty," she said crisply. "It's a reminder."

That stopped me.

She exhaled, setting her papers aside. "That case belonged to one of the finest examples of Navarro-style ceremonial carving. A figure used in ancestral rites—not made for sale. Spiraled eyes, flared cheekbones, lacquered fangs. Wings. Irreplaceable."

My thoughts flashed back to the jaguar figure I'd seen in the mercado.

"So... what happened to it?"

"It was taken," she said. "Years ago. Under mysterious circumstances."

My gaze darted back to the bare velvet mount. "And the museum kept the plaque? All this time?"

"I've had to argue with the trustees for every centimeter of wall space it takes up. It was important. I want people to see what we've lost. These pieces don't just disappear—they're stolen. Sold to collectors who treat cultural heritage like souvenir baubles." Her voice went flat. "It sends me into a murderous rage sometimes."

I blinked. "Wow. That's... vivid."

She straightened, smoothing her blouse. "Sorry. I meant... deep frustration."

"Sure," I said. "Is that how you felt about Curtis Vale?"

She didn't answer right away.

Then, finally, she said, "It's how I'd feel about anyone who treated our heritage like a cheap tourist trinket."

"Most of the trustees still think me a fool," she said, tone hardening.

A furrow creased my forehead. "Why?"

"Because, unlike Don Abel, they think it foolish to save space for something the fire consumed."

"The winged jaguar perished in the fire?"

"That's what everyone believes. Personally, I think Curtis Vale may have arranged for that fire to be set and for the jaguar to conveniently disappear."

"He was operating even back then?"

She sneered. "Men like him are like *las cucarachas*, the cockroaches. They never go away."

I let the silence stretch between us—let it dry and settle, like plaster that won't hold. Then I said, lightly and clearly, "So, if this piece was that important, why wasn't it protected?"

Soledad stilled. Not a dramatic freeze—just a quiet suspension. Like breath caught in the chest, unwilling to be let out.

She didn't look up. Just brushed her fingers along the edge of a file folder, aligning the corners that were already aligned.

"I tried," she said, finally.

I leaned forward slightly. "Tried how?"

A pause. Then—an exhale, half frustration, half defeat. "I filed a cultural protection claim. It would've granted the piece official designation—made it part of the national record. Unmovable. Unexportable. Untouchable."

"But...?"

"I filed it three days before the fire."

Her voice was soft. Her words cracked like kindling.

I blinked. "Three days?"

She nodded.

"And then the workshop burned down. The jaguar vanished."

Another nod.

"That's... incredibly coincidental."

Soledad met my gaze for the first time in the last five minutes. There was something steely in her eyes now—not anger. Not guilt. Just the weary burn of someone who'd carried the truth a little too long without backup.

"I know how it sounds," she said. "But I filed the paperwork. I made the call. It was supposed to be safe."

"Do you have proof?"

"I kept the stamped copy," she said. "Even when they told me it must've gotten lost. That it never reached the registry office. I kept mine."

Something hard twisted in my chest.

"Do you think Vale intercepted it?"

"I think he made it disappear… just like the *jaguar*."

We stood there, two women staring across a chasm that looked like paperwork and arson. Something nibbled at by brain and told me it was a lot more like motive.

CARVING OUT THE TRUTH

I spent most of the rest of the day typing up the outline for my article in The Wandering Foodie. Lizzie and Mozzie were still snoring in the bed.

The sun had dropped just enough to gild the market stalls in warm amber light by the time they popped awake, but not enough to cool the air. After a much-needed potty break for my Schnoodle, Lizzie and I wandered through the lighter afternoon crowd—less chaos, more browsing, fewer elbows to the ribs.

"Come on, Mozzie. Let's get going," I called to Mozart, who was busy sniffing at a melted *paleta*. He quickly abandoned it, with maybe a little reluctance, and trotted alongside us, tail high, sniffing everything like he'd taken it upon himself to be the olfactory cataloguer of Oaxaca.

Lizzie stopped at a stall that specialized in festival jewelry—earrings shaped like sugar skulls, miniature *milagros*, even a pair that looked like tiny *cempasúchil* blooms preserved in resin.

"Oh my God," she whispered, holding up a pair of jaguar-head studs. "These say I'm festive *and* feral."

"You say that enough without earrings."

"I need them."

I let her fawn and flirt with the vendor while I kept my eyes just a little east of the baubles. Catalina's stall was in view, tucked under the awning with her usual particularity—carefully arranged carvings, a trio of jaguar figures, and her sketchbook angled just out of reach.

She was restocking a shelf when it happened.

A tourist—tall, loud, and sunburnt in the way only the overconfident ever are—raised a bulky camera and snapped three photos in quick succession, flash on full blast.

Catalina's posture snapped straight.

"*¡Señor!*" she barked, stepping out from behind the booth. "You do *not* take photos without permission."

Her voice wasn't shrill. It was iron.

The man blinked, flustered. "It's just for my blog—"

"No," she said firmly. "*Ask first.* Always."

Lizzie turned to me, eyebrows halfway to her hairline. "Well. That was quite a vibe."

I didn't answer. I was too focused on Catalina's stance—protective, not performative. She'd moved instinctively. Not to defend her stall. To guard something *within* it. I had no idea what.

The mercado had thinned, the afternoon sun casting long shadows that sharpened every corner and curve of the artisan stalls. A breeze pushed through the square, rustling papel picado like whispered secrets. Lizzie was off making a production of comparing two nearly identical earrings shaped like skeleton tacos—Mozart seated loyally at her feet like her snacking consigliere.

I should've been charmed by the moment. Something tugged my attention sideways. It was Catalina.

She stood at the far end of her stall, not carving, not chatting—just...watching. Her body was angled oddly, as if listening without being seen listening. Her eyes scanned left, then right, then down the length of the narrow street that led behind the vendors' stalls. She pulled something small from the back table and slipped it into the woven tote at her side.

Nothing about the gesture was dramatic. And maybe that's why it set the hairs on my arm tingling.

Catalina reached for a wooden placard, flipped it to ***cerrado***, and then pulled the curtain flap down on her stall. Not even a glance around to see who might be watching.

Except I was.

She moved quickly—but not with purpose. It was more like her feet knew where they were going, and the rest of her hadn't caught up yet. Her shoulders rounded forward under the weight of something internal. And then she disappeared into the narrow alley behind the market, swallowed by the shade of overhanging balconies and tangled bougainvillea.

I didn't think. I just followed. Not because I thought she was about to confess something—though part of me hoped she might. It was a possibility. No one hunches their shoulders like that unless they're carrying something too heavy to walk with… and no one should have to carry it alone.

Not even suspects.

The alley curved gently, the noise of the mercado muffled behind adobe walls and dangling cords of drying laundry. The deeper I went, the more the world quieted—like I'd stepped through the back of a tapestry into a part of the city not meant for tourists.

"Catalina," I called, not loud, not demanding. Just enough to be heard over the rustle of her footsteps.

She slowed.

Didn't stop. Not at first.

Then she did—one sandal scuffing to a halt on the cobbled path, her shoulders rising in a long inhale before she let it go all at once. She didn't turn around.

"If you're here to ask more questions," she said, voice low and clear, "ask them now. I'm too tired to pretend."

Her tone wasn't bitter. It wasn't even wary. It was worn. Like someone whose skin didn't fit right anymore.

I didn't answer right away. Just took a few slow steps forward until there were only a few feet of shaded air between us. I could smell paint—fresh and citrusy—and something else. Copal, maybe.

"Then I won't pretend either," I said. "I didn't follow you to interrogate you. I just… saw you leave and thought you looked like someone who might want to be followed."

She let out a sound—part laugh, part sigh. Still no turn.

That's when I heard them behind me. Mozart's paws clicked softly on the stone. Lizzie's sandals shuffled with considerably less subtlety. She caught up to me, half-breathless.

"We're not eavesdropping," she said brightly. "Just… morally adjacent."

Mozart sat calmly alert.

Catalina finally turned. And in her eyes, I saw something I wasn't ready for. Not guilt. Not even fear. Just someone who was finally, completely, heartbreakingly tired of holding it all in.

Catalina sank onto the low stone wall like her legs had been holding up more than just her body. The light caught the edges of her cheekbones, sharp from weeks of tension. Here, however, in the hush of the alley, they seemed softened. She didn't look at me. Her gaze wandered somewhere past my shoulder, into a place I couldn't follow.

Mozart sat beside her, tail sweeping once, then still.

"He said we could leave it all behind," she said softly. "The market. The rules. The expectations. All of it." Her fingers drifted to her stomach—not dramatically, not staged. Just… a small, unconscious brush, like muscle memory from a thought that lived deeper than words.

Curtis Vale's name didn't need to be spoken again. It was already there, a ghost between us, puffing out the dust with every shallow breath.

"He told me he wanted something real. A life with me." Her voice wasn't wistful. It wasn't even bitter. Just tired. "He made me believe it. Like I was more than a mark. More than a name on a stall."

Lizzie, still quiet for once, crouched down near Mozart, one hand resting on his back like she wasn't entirely sure whether it was to comfort the dog or herself.

"I gave him sketches," Catalina continued. "Not all of them. Just... enough. Enough to feel like I was letting him into my world." She blinked once, then looked up—directly at me. "And then I found out he'd already left it. Long before he said goodbye."

My throat went tight. Because this wasn't just betrayal. This was an invasion. Curtis hadn't just stolen her trust. He'd stolen her future. And Catalina was still picking up the pieces.

"He said my hands were magic."

Catalina's voice didn't rise. It didn't break apart with drama or spill out in a rush. It just... thinned. Like paper held over flame—warped around the edges while still trying to hold its shape.

I didn't speak. Neither did Lizzie. Even Mozzie seemed to hold still, ears flicking toward her like he understood this wasn't the moment for sniffing or sneezing.

Catalina looked down at her fingers—slender, calloused, nicked in places by tools that demanded more than most people could give. "He said I had something the rest of the world had forgotten how to touch. That if we left, really left, he'd make sure I was seen. In galleries. In papers. On walls where people paid to understand what they were looking at."

She swallowed. I caught the flash of something behind her eyes—pride and shame, tangled up in a way that looked too familiar.

"He said he'd protect me from everything," she continued, her voice barely above a breath. Her fingers curled slightly over her stomach again. And then her gaze lifted to mine, sharp and flat like water just before it freezes. "I had no idea I needed to protect myself from *him*."

I felt that one like a dropped chisel—devastatingly quiet.

Lizzie reached into her bag and handed Catalina a tissue without a word. And for once, the market noise behind us faded completely. Because sometimes betrayal doesn't come with shouting. It comes with silence. And broken promises carved too deep to sand away.

Catalina didn't speak for a while. Her fingers wrapped around the strap of the canvas tote like it was the only thing tethering her to the ground.

"I was working on something for my father," she said, her voice nearly lost in the buzz of the mercado behind us. "Something I thought might… prove I was worthy of the family style."

I waited, silent.

"I knew he'd never give me his blessing," she continued. "Not after the fire. I thought if I could just show him I understood… that I respected it… maybe that would be enough."

She glanced down at the bag. Not dramatically. Just a quick glance of her eyes. A tell.

"The winged jaguar," I affirmed.

Catalina shook her head. "No. Not that. This was something else."

Lizzie leaned in just a touch. "What's in the bag?"

Catalina's grip tightened. "I carved it in secret," she said, almost to herself. "The same design. I used every reference I had. Every sketch I remembered. I spent hours at the museum studying the old pieces."

Lizzie started to say something. I held up a warning hand.

Finally, Catalina's shoulders slumped. She slipped one, long-fingered hand into the tote and drew out the winged jaguar figure—the same one I had seen earlier in the market!

I drew in a slow breath. "That's what Curtis saw?"

Catalina's silence answered for her.

"I thought he was impressed," she whispered. "I thought he wanted to help me share it. Protect it. Instead..." Her eyes burned. "He sold it without asking. Called it his discovery." She sniffled. "Didn't mention me at all."

And just like that, the truth settled between us. He hadn't just stolen something sacred. He'd stripped it of identity. Of lineage. Of name. That jaguar in her bag? It wasn't a carving.

It was a wound.

I kept my voice soft. "Does your father know?"

Catalina's breath hitched—not dramatically, just enough to draw a line between before and after. She looked down at her hands, thumbs rubbing the fabric of the tote in her lap.

"I told him everything," she said finally. "When I found out what Curtis had done—how he stole the winged jaguar I had made, turned our family's totem into something cheap for a collector—I ran home."

She paused, chewing the inside of her cheek. "I was upset. Angry. Stupid, maybe. I made the mistake of telling him everything. About Curtis. About the jaguar. About... the baby."

Even Lizzie stilled beside me. No quip. No flutter. Just silence.

Catalina's voice thinned. "He didn't say a word. Just stood there. Then he walked over to the carving knife I'd been using—one of his old ones, the good ones—and he snapped it in half against the floor."

My brows lifted. "He broke the blade?"

She nodded. "Like it didn't deserve to survive what I'd used it for. Splinters went everywhere."

Lizzie winced. "Okay, that's… intense."

Catalina didn't flinch. "He told me never to speak Curtis's name again. To never honor it. Not with my voice. Not with my hands."

There it was—anger, grief, shame—all braided into the silence that had hung between them at the house. It was over so much more than Curtis's betrayal. It was over how Catalina had chosen, however briefly, to believe in him.

And how Don Abel never could.

I let a few seconds pass—just long enough for the weight of her last words to settle between us.

"So," I said slowly, "Curtis was trying to pawn your copy off as the original Navarro *yaguar*?"

Catalina nodded once. No hesitation. Just grim certainty.

My brow furrowed. "Then what was the small jaguar figure in the *mercado*? I saw one. Navarro colors. Navarro markings. Spiral eyes, that signature red-orange—the whole thing. It looked real."

Catalina's mouth tightened, but she didn't flinch. "I am a Navarro," she said. "Despite what my father believes, the jaguar has always kept our family strong. Even when the fire tried to burn us out, even when grief tried to silence us, it was still there."

She exhaled slowly, like the words had been waiting years to surface. "Curtis thought he could take that—turn it into something he could sell. So, I decided to take it back."

Lizzie tilted her head, watching her carefully. "By making a copy?"

"By making many," Catalina said. "If he wanted to claim

he had found 'the one,' I would give the world a hundred. A thousand. Enough that no collector could ever say which was real."

I blinked. "So, the jaguar I saw?"

"I was working on it at my stall," she admitted. "I think Curtis saw it. I got nervous—moved it into the wares of a fellow artisan for safekeeping. Someone I trust. I didn't want him to take that from me, too."

She looked down, not ashamed—*resolute*.

"You can steal a carving," she whispered. "You cannot steal what it stands for."

Catalina stood slowly, dusting the hem of her skirt like she was brushing off more than just dirt. Her shoulders squared—with defiance.

"You have your answers," she said, her voice stripped of ornament. "Or enough of them to twist into whatever you need." It wasn't bitter. It wasn't even sharp. Just tired. And true. She didn't wait for a reply. Just turned and walked back the way she came, disappearing down the narrow path between stalls, her bag slung over one shoulder like an accusation she'd decided not to hurl. I didn't follow.

Lizzie was quiet beside me. Mozart sniffed the air, then sat down with a soft whuff, as if he, too, had nothing left to add.

A breeze curled around the edge of the alley, and with it came the faintest whiff of something scorched—singed wood, maybe. Or memory. I stared after Catalina, the spiral from her sketch still looping in my head. It wasn't just a motif. It was a wound, curling inward, never quite closing. A story that wouldn't stop telling itself. Love. Loss. Legacy. A winged *yaguar*. And a silence heavy enough to bury truth.

We stood there for a moment longer, letting the market bustle swell back around us.

Lizzie cleared her throat. "Do you think she killed him,"

she asked. "If you ask me, I really wouldn't blame her. He really was a first class louse."

"I don't know," I whispered.

Lizzie scowled as she watched me chew my bottom lip. "You know," she started, "I recommend a *churro* if you're *that* hungry."

I rolled my eyes.

"Seriously," Lizzie continued. "*Gato* got your tongue?"

I shook my head. "No. I was just thinking."

She snorted. "I thought I smelled something burning."

I whacked her in the shoulder. "I'm being serious!"

She held her hands up in defense. "Okay, okay! What's on your mind?"

"Curtis was trying to pass off Catalina's work as the original winged Navarro *yaguar*."

"And?"

"Well, it doesn't make sense. Soledad told me she thought Curtis engineered the theft of the original Navarrao *yaguar*. She thinks he might have had something to do with the original fire. If he had the original, like Soledad suspected, why would he need a fake?"

"You're right." Then, Lizzie's face puckered. "Darcy, if he caused the fire that burned down Don Abel's shop... that would make him way worse than a thief."

My eyes widened as I arrived at the same conclusion. I thought of Don Abel's scarred hands—the ones he had used to carry the charred remains of his daughter out of the burning shop.

"That would make him a murderer," Lizzie whispered.

Had Soledad shared her suspicions with Don Abel? If so, had he come to the same conclusion we just had? His words at the *hacienda* floated back to the top of my mind.

Not without blessing... or blood.

DINNERS AND DEDUCTIONS

By the time we got back to the hotel, my brain felt like a pot of over-reduced *mole*—thick, dark, and dangerously close to burning. Too many details. Too many suspects. Too many spirals—literal and figurative. Lizzie had hopped down to the lobby to see if they could mail a postcard for her.

I kicked off my sandals and collapsed backward onto the bedspread at *Casa de las Bugambilias*. The fabric was sun-faded cotton, hand-stitched in deep purples and reds, and smelled faintly of clean linen, *cempasúchil*, and the sweet woody tang of the bougainvillea that climbed the window grille outside. The ceiling fan above me spun in slow, deliberate circles—just like my thoughts. Relentless, rhythmic, useless.

The case wasn't just tangled anymore—it was braided. Motives wrapped in secrets, twisted with guilt, tradition, and a generation's worth of grief. There were too many pieces. Too many jaguars.

Catalina. Hurt. Haunted. But not entirely off the hook. Don Abel? Capable of wrath, yes—but not chaos. His anger was a burn, not a flash. Molina? All slither and silk and sidesteps. No artistry. He couldn't carve his way out of a wooden box, much less replicate a sacred totem.

Then there was María. Or Lucia. I still wasn't sure what name belonged to the truth.

And Soledad Pineda...

I sat up, heartbeat tapping against the base of my throat.

Dr. Pineda had secrets, too. She'd fought to keep that jaguar plaque mounted long after the carving vanished. She'd practically hissed when I brought up Vale. She'd mentioned a splinter—"a hazard of the job." The more I pondered it, the more I suspected it hadn't come from a crate of dusty archives. Maybe it came from something more recent. More forbidden.

Was she the ghost I hadn't seen clearly? The one hiding in plain sight?

A knock at the door pulled me back. Two quick raps. Then a familiar hum.

Lizzie.

She strolled in like she was headlining a musical set in colonial Oaxaca. Her camera hung around her neck. I assumed she had been out taking photos. I was about to find out that wasn't one hundred percent true.

"You need to stop thinking," she announced, already dropping her purse onto the chair with the floral cushion that creaked when you breathed near it.

"Thinking is literally my job," I quipped. "Of course, it's usually about food."

"Thinking," she replied, flopping down beside me, "is what's keeping you from sleeping. Or smiling. Or enjoying the fact that your best friend bought Mozzie a marigold-themed collar that he now hates with the heat of a thousand suns."

I looked over the side of the bed. Mozart lay flat on the

cool terra-cotta tile like a dog who had seen too much. The tiny golden-orange silk flowers woven into his collar had crumpled under the force of his sheer disdain. He gave a long, exasperated sigh.

"I see you're both thriving," I said.

"Fine," Lizzie chirped. "You don't want to smile? Name one thing that'll distract you."

I lifted a brow. "From a tangled web of cultural betrayal, possible murder, and stolen heritage? That's a tall order."

She grinned like the cat that stole my suspect board.

"Oh, that's easy. Food. And Marcus Evans."

I blinked. "Please tell me you're joking."

"Not even a little. One of them is downstairs."

I sat up straighter. "Which one?"

She gave me the infuriating smile of a woman who knew too much and loved it. "Guess."

"Lizzie…"

"Do you want to change into something cute or do you want to overheat in that wrinkled linen and pretend you're not totally into the emotionally unavailable secret agent?"

I muttered something impolite into a throw pillow.

Mozart barked once.

"That's what I thought," Lizzie said, already heading for the door. "He said to meet him at the gate. Mozzie and I will be fine." She waved a hand. "There's a cute guy down at the front desk. I'm going to go pick his brain about some good places for photos."

The door closed behind her with the faint clink of the brass handle. I stood, brushed a hand through my hair, and told myself I was only going downstairs for the food.

A fonda. The word lingered in my head like cinnamon in the air.

And somehow, I already knew the taste of the lie I was telling myself.

Marcus was waiting just outside the painted gate, sleeves rolled and collar unbuttoned, a little sweat at his temples catching the last light of day like he'd stepped out of a noir novel and straight into my unresolved feelings. He looked like a man who hadn't quite adjusted to the heat.

Or to me.

"I found us a *fonda*," he said, as casually as if he'd picked a playlist.

I arched my brow. "You know what a *fonda* is?"

Marcus shrugged, all dry ease and travel fatigue. "I asked the woman at the desk where you'd go if you were trying to avoid tourists, overpriced *mezcal*, and being seen. She handed me a post-it with two names. This one came with three exclamation marks."

I didn't say anything. Mostly because my stomach did it for me.

We slipped through the plaza before the night's music had fully taken hold—past quiet doorways and crumbling stone walls bathed in the gold-pink wash of magic hour. The street smelled like woodsmoke and citrus peel. My sandals scuffed against the uneven stone, the rhythm just a half-beat behind his.

It wasn't far. Nothing ever is in Oaxaca if your feet and your heart are in the right place.

The *fonda* didn't announce itself. No neon. No sidewalk chalkboard with tired puns. Just a low-slung lime-washed courtyard tucked behind a crooked gate and framed in flowering vines. Tin lanterns illuminated the archways, their light caught in the glossy green leaves above.

And the scent. *Dios mío.*

The scent was a quiet promise: charred tomatoes, caramelized onion, woodsmoke and lime leaves. Fresh tortillas puffing on a clay comal. Someone, somewhere, had been toasting dried chiles just long enough to coax out their soul.

In Oaxaca, a *fonda* is not a restaurant.

It's a declaration. A home wrapped in aroma and memory, where generations of women have passed down secrets in sauce and cured clay. It's where tomatoes are roasted until they give up the ghost, where garlic is charred to confession, where masa is not measured in grams but in instinct.

The woman at the front gave us a warm nod—no menu, no fuss, just a gentle wave toward a cluster of mismatched wooden tables nestled beneath a bloom-heavy bougainvillea. The chairs were scuffed. The floor was stone. The tablecloths were simple.

Marcus let me choose the table.

I chose the one nearest the open kitchen window—where I could see the flash of a *molcajete* grinding something red and glistening into surrender. A slow ladle of broth caught the light and glowed.

I didn't speak. I didn't have to. This was the kind of place that asked you to listen first. To the sizzle. To the scrape of a spoon against a pot. To the breath of woodsmoke winding between shadows.

And in that quiet, Marcus pulled out the chair for me. And I let him. A shy smile broke across my face.

The first course arrived in mismatched clayware still warm from the fire—plates that had lived lives before this one, each rim chipped in its own honest way. The tamales were swaddled in banana leaves so dark and glossy they looked lacquered, their folds steamed soft around parcels of *masa*.

I unwrapped mine slowly. My eyes drifting to Marcus's face. "You know, you never cease to surprise me."

"What do you mean?"

I gestured. “How you always seem to know what I need—sometimes before I do. I was starving. And, out of nowhere, you show up and take me to this place.” I paused. My voice dropped to a near whisper. “It’s like we’re…”

“… two parts of the same whole?” His voice sounded husky, laden with emotion. The silence hung heavy between us for a moment, then I cleared my throat.

“Let’s see what deliciousness is in here!” I redirected my attention to the contents of the banana leaves.

Inside were *tamales oaxaqueños,* thick and dense and smudged with *mole negro* so rich it didn’t taste like chocolate or spice or even smoke—it tasted like a memory. Dark, layered, a little bitter, and entirely sacred. The kind of sauce that didn’t whisper flavor so much as a confession of tastes. Cinnamon, clove, burnt tortilla, toasted sesame, raisins, and the slow shadow of dried chiles all playing in time.

I took one bite. Closed my eyes. And dropped my fork.

“Don’t speak,” I said, hands frozen mid-prayer over the plate. “Let me die here.”

Marcus made a sound that was half laugh, half reverence. “Do I at least get to eat first?”

I cracked one eye open and pointed a warning finger. “Fine. If you say *‘mmm’* out loud, though, I’m throwing you in the fountain.”

He grinned and picked up his fork—using it correctly, which earned him points I would not be publicly awarding.

“Do you know what your next assignment is?” Marcus asked as we ate.

“Why? You looking to coordinate your next case?” I chuckled.

“Just a little curious as to where the next body’s going to drop.”

I grimaced. “Yeah. I do seem to be a magnet for that sort of thing." I popped another bite of tamale into my mouth and chewed thoughtfully. I swallowed before I spoke again. "Pretty soon, people are going to start looking at *me* like a suspect."

"Never!" Marcus beamed widely. The expression sent a flood of warmth through my chest. I loved that smile.

Then, I shook my head. "Actually, I'm headed home for the Thanksgiving holidays this year."

"Ah. The American excuse to stuff yourselves silly, then sit comatosed on the sofa watching a sport that calls itself 'football' but is no such thing."

I playfully stuck out my tongue. "Mom's been begging me —no, *insisting* I come home this year. Something she says she *needs* to talk to me about."

"Sounds serious."

"I doubt it. She probably just wants someone else to do the cooking this year. Catherine Grace Finnegan is a hard woman to say no to, so..."

The next course arrived steaming in a deep terracotta bowl. *Caldo de piedra*—stone soup, Oaxacan-style. A clear, fragrant broth poured over raw river fish, tomatoes, onions, fresh herbs, and slivers of chile, with a still-sizzling river stone dropped in at the last second to cook it table-side. The scent rose immediately—earthy, clean, elemental.

Marcus watched the steam rise in ribbons. He peered into the bowl, then looked at me. "That's a rock in there."

"Correct," I replied, leaning in to inhale the delicate perfume. "A lava stone. Heated until it glows, then dropped into the broth. It's Zapotec. Men used to make it on the riverbank, only for women and elders. Sacred, not showy."

He dipped his spoon in carefully. "And now?"

"Now it's dinner. And it's perfect."

The broth was subtle. Bright from tomato, rounded by the slickness of chile oil, and touched with the faintest kiss of mineral heat from the stone. The fish flaked like it had been waiting its whole life to be understood.

Around us, the *fonda* breathed. Low laughter. The clink of clay mugs. The scent of garlic crisping in oil from someone else's plate. Somewhere nearby, a baby cooed and someone scolded a cat in rapid Spanish. A lime wedge thunked gently into a glass.

For one moment, just one, the case slipped to the edges of my mind. Vale. Catalina. Soledad. The jaguar. All of it softened. Not forgotten. Never forgotten. Just… set aside.

Just long enough to feel something warm in my hands again.

By the time the *estofado* arrived—a fall-apart chicken swimming in a *mole amarillo* so thick it clung to the back of the spoon like a secret—I'd almost managed to forget about the case.

Almost.

The sauce was rich with toasted seeds and the faintest sweetness of ripe plantains, its golden hue deepened by cinnamon and garlic and something just a touch smoky—like it had kissed the edge of a fire before deciding to stay civilized. The chicken practically fell apart at the press of a fork. A ring of roasted plantains fanned out beside it like a halo.

I took a bite, chewed slowly, then sighed.

"This is criminal," I muttered. "This should be illegal."

Marcus chuckled, breaking off a piece of warm tortilla and using it to scoop up sauce like he'd been raised on it. "You say that about every dish in every country."

"I mean it every time."

The candle between us flickered as someone opened the courtyard door, letting in a brief gust of night air laced with woodsmoke. Shadows danced on the stone walls around us. At another table, someone laughed too loudly. A guitarist struck up a gentle tune. And for a second, the tension in my shoulders eased.

Then I looked at my plate.

And I remembered.

"I still don't know," I said finally, spearing a roasted plantain with more aggression than it deserved. "Every suspect had a motive. Most had opportunities. None of it *clicks.* You know that feeling when something just *clicks*? And until then, your brain's like a scratched record?"

Marcus nodded slowly, chewing. He wiped the corner of his mouth with his napkin before speaking. "Who stands out to you?"

I looked up from my plate. "Funny you should say that."

He leaned forward, just slightly, the candlelight catching in his eyes.

"I keep thinking about Soledad. She's been helpful. Smart. Guarded. Lately..." I trailed off, choosing my words. "Something shifted. The plaque for the missing Navarro piece. The way she's protected it like a vigil, even though the actual jaguar has been gone for years. She said she fought with the trustees to keep the display up—just to make sure people didn't forget."

"That sounds... passionate."

"It was more than that," I said, picking up my water glass. I din't drink. "She said it sent her into a *murderous rage* when people treated heritage like a cheap souvenir."

I let the words hang there, watching Marcus for a reaction. He didn't blink.

"I've heard worse motives," he said simply, voice low. Measured.

I set my glass down. "Exactly."

He didn't interrupt as I recapped the pieces out loud—the timeline of Curtis Vale's arrival, his connections to the missing jaguar carving, the Interpol investigation into smuggling, and Soledad's quiet fury. I told him about the splinter, too—how she'd casually picked at it when we visited the museum, how she'd brushed it off as the hazard of handling "old things."

"She said it like it was normal," I murmured. "I'm telling you, it wasn't just a splinter. It was red. Bright. Fresh. Navarro orange, maybe."

Marcus's brows lifted slightly.

"She works with old textiles. Paper archives. Clay plaques at most," I added. "There's nothing in her job that would explain a splinter from freshly carved wood. Not unless she was somewhere she shouldn't have been. Or handling something she shouldn't have touched."

He didn't say anything at first—just turned his fork slowly in the pool of *mole*. Thoughtful. Calculating.

I pushed on. "You said Interpol suspected Curtis was laundering real pieces by passing them off as 'inspired by' knockoffs. What if Soledad found out he had the jaguar carving—maybe even saw him with it—and he blew her off? Treated her like just another museum bureaucrat?"

"She's no bureaucrat," Marcus said, with something close to admiration. "Not from what you've told me."

"No," I agreed. "She's a guardian. One of the last who cares enough to fight for things that are supposed to matter. To protect what's sacred. And Curtis…"

"Curtis was everything she hated," Marcus finished for me. "Charm without roots. Flash without respect. A collector's ego in a country he didn't understand."

"He was her worst-case scenario wrapped in linen and pretense," I said softly.

We sat with that for a moment, the candle between us dimming like it might go out just to give us some privacy.

I wasn't sure what Marcus was thinking. I knew what *I* was thinking, though..

Curtis had hurt a lot of people. Lied to more. Soledad Pineda was another kettle of fish. She didn't strike me as someone who *forgave* things like cultural betrayal. And if she'd seen what he was doing, if she'd tried to stop it—filed paperwork, warned people, spoken out—and he'd ignored her? She might've decided it was time to make a louder statement.

Beside me, Marcus reached for a small wooden bowl of salt and hissed softly.

"What?" I asked, already halfway too concerned.

He looked down at his palm. "Splinter."

He held up his hand. Just beneath the pad of his thumb, something sharp and thin protruded from his skin—red-orange, like a matchstick shaved down to a dagger.

Without thinking, I reached for him. "Let me."

He didn't move as I gently took his hand in mine, turned it toward the dim candlelight, and plucked the splinter free with two fingers. It came loose with a tiny hiss of resistance. I held it between my fingers. A sliver of red-orange wood—almost too vivid for something that wasn't trying to be seen. Not just paint. Pigment soaked so deep into the grain it could've been blood.

The *alebrije* at the mercado—splintered. Soledad's hand. My breath caught.

"What is it?" Marcus asked, eyes narrowing.

And suddenly, something clicked. It wasn't loud. If definitely wasn't certain. Just… an itch of recognition.

Dr. Soledad Pineda. Who spoke about Navarro carvings with reverence so fierce it bordered on familial. Who protected plaques like they were altars. Who had a *splinter* in her finger the last time I saw her. A splinter from what? I swallowed.

"Darcy," Marcus said, tone low but direct. "Where did you just go?"

I blinked. "Nowhere."

Even as I said it, my mind wasn't convinced.

Because Catalina had said Lucia Navarro was gone. But, so much about Dr. Pineda suddenly felt like a woman trying to keep a name buried. Not lost. Protected. And if Soledad Pineda wasn't just a museum worker…

Then maybe she wasn't the only one keeping secrets.

I looked at the tiny sliver of wood between my fingers. "I think," I said slowly, "we need to go see Dr. Pineda again. Tomorrow."

Because Curtis Vale may have stolen art. I was beginning to think Soledad Pineda might have stolen justice.

SPLINTERED SUSPECTS

Marcus met Lizzie and me for an early breakfast at the hotel. I'm not certain who yawned more loudly—her or Mozart—as we informed her of our plans to go to the *Museo de las Culturas* and question Soledad.

We got to the museum just after opening—too early for tourists, too late for plausible deniability.

The massive wooden doors gave way with a reluctant groan, and the scent of old limestone, beeswax polish, and long-settled history curled into my nose. Still, the air felt… different. Not quite musty. Not quite sacred. Just off. Like the building had exhaled something it hadn't meant to.

The last time we were here, I'd felt a hush of reverence. A cathedral of culture and curation. This morning, it felt more like we were stepping into a courtroom—and not on the jury side.

Our footsteps echoed across the tile, swallowed quickly by the thick adobe walls and arched ceilings above. The shafts of sunlight streaking through the clerestory windows were the same—diffused gold on stone. Even those felt subdued, like the museum itself was holding its breath.

Marcus walked beside me, his hands tucked in his pockets, shirt sleeves rolled to the elbow. No badge. No notebook. Just him in diplomat mode, which was still somehow more intimidating than most interrogators I'd met. He hadn't said much over breakfast—just a quiet confirmation that yes, it was time to talk to Soledad. And no, we weren't bringing backup.

Lizzie had bowed out cheerfully over a second cup of *café de olla.* "I need to take some pictures and I may have promised Mozart we'd take some selfies. And maybe not accuse anyone of murder for a whole hour," she'd added. "But text me if someone confesses."

So, it was just us. Just me and the man who knew when to let silence do the talking—and the museum that suddenly felt a little more defensive than curated. I wasn't sure who was on trial.

I had a feeling we were about to find out.

We found her near the side entrance, in the long corridor that led toward the archive wing. The light here was thinner, filtered through old glass panes that warped the view of the courtyard outside. Dust floated in the air, dancing sparkles.

Dr. Pineda was speaking to someone. Quietly. Firmly.

It took a second to place him—not because I didn't know him, but because I hadn't expected him *here.*

Gerardo Molina. That red cane was unmistakable. My head tilted without thinking.

That *chipped* red cane—a detail I had missed in our previous encounters.

Molina must have felt our approach—either that or he spotted Marcus first. He muttered something clipped and final to Soledad, turned on his heel, and slipped through the side door before we'd crossed halfway through the gallery. No glance back. No farewell.

Just gone.

The heavy door clicked shut behind him.

Soledad didn't turn right away. She stood there a beat longer, one hand still lightly resting on the edge of the flat file drawers like she needed a prop to finish the scene. When she finally faced us, her blouse was crisp and precise, sleeves rolled to just below the elbow, her collar buttoned all the way up like she'd armor-plated herself in cotton.

Her expression didn't shift. No welcome. No annoyance. Just ready. The kind of ready that tells you the conversation ahead isn't going to surprise her. Marcus gave her a polite nod. I stayed quiet.

Dr. Pineda smoothed the drawer handle once with her thumb—reflex, not nerves—and stepped back.

"Miss Finnegan," she drawled, looking long and appreciatively at Marcus. "And a guest."

I must admit, my belly did a strange little flop. I tried to gather my thoughts before she looked back at me.

"I did not expect to see you again. You are becoming quite the connoisseur of Oaxacan art. I only wish more people shared your appreciation."

"Unfortunately, we're not here for a tour," I replied. I gestured to Marcus. "This is Marcus Evans. *Agent* Marcus Evans. From Interpol."

Dr. Pineda's forehead wrinkled for a fraction of a second, then smoothed. She nodded once. "Then I suppose we should begin."

I offered a thin smile. "I just had a few follow-up questions. About the exhibit. Museum-related."

The kind of polite lie that leaves enough air between the words for the truth to breathe.

Marcus remained just behind me—still, silent, measured.

Diplomat mode. Which was, if I was being honest, about four degrees more unnerving than when he went full Interpol.

Dr. Pineda didn't flinch. She simply closed the folio drawer with an elegance that made the movement feel ceremonial. The sound was soft, but final. Like something being tucked away for good.

"I'm happy to help," she said. "And call me Soledad."

The suggestion wasn't friendly. She clearly stated it as though she were giving us *permission*. Everything in her posture—shoulders square, chin slightly lifted—screamed defensive. She wasn't worried about being caught off guard. She was worried about being *right.*

I glanced down at the brass plaque beneath the drawer. A brief history of the archive's acquisitions etched in official language—neutral, sterile, reverent. A thought occurred to me. History didn't live in plaques. It lived in people. In the gaps. In what they refused to say.

Soledad's silence wasn't passive. It was defiant. And the way she stood there, spine aligned with the marble pillars, made one thing perfectly clear. She wasn't waiting to be questioned. She was waiting to see if we had the nerve to ask.

I shifted my weight slightly, letting my voice go casual—just enough warmth to feel conversational. "How long have you worked here, Soledad?"

Soledad didn't blink. "Several years."

The answer came too quickly. Too polished. Like a line rehearsed more than lived.

I nodded slowly, tracing a fingertip along the edge of the archival drawer. "Have you always lived in Oaxaca?"

There. A flicker of unease.

She held still—just a breath too long. Her eyes, previously anchored with that museum-grade steadiness, slid to the window, where the first shaft of late morning light spilled through panes flecked with age.

"No," she said at last. "I haven't been back long. I was born here. Life circumstances took me elsewhere at a young age."

My gaze narrowed slightly. That word again. *Circumstances.* Vague. Muted. The kind of word people used when the truth had teeth.

Behind me, Marcus didn't move a muscle. I could feel his attention sharpen like a lens being focused. He'd caught it too.

"What kind of circumstances?" I asked, gentler this time. Not pressing. Just opening the door to see if she'd walk through.

Soledad's hands smoothed the hem of her blouse—one motion, crisp and contained. "Family. Work. Both."

"That's a long absence," I said, meeting her eyes. "To be away from a place like this. And then come back."

Her chin lifted slightly. "Some places don't let you go. Even when you try."

A silence settled between us. Not heavy. Taut. Woven with something older than suspicion. Something closer to sorrow.

Who leaves Oaxaca—its colors, its ghosts, its stories—and returns after years away just to guard the bones of what was lost? And what brings them back?

It wasn't just history she was protecting. It was something more personal. More broken. And possibly… more incriminating.

Marcus shifted, his voice smooth and even. It was edged with something deliberate.

"Where were you the night Curtis Vale was killed?"

No accusation. No tilt in his tone. Just an open space waiting to be filled.

Soledad didn't step into it. She *stilled.* Her back straightened as if on instinct. Her jaw flexed. It was the kind of restraint that spoke of long practice.

She didn't answer right away. Instead, she turned her gaze toward the arched window, where filtered light cut across the floor in honeyed ribbons. A long breath. Measured. Intentional.

"I was at the *mercado*," she said at last.

Not defensive. Not rattled. Just... precise.

She gave a single, definitive nod. "At my booth. Or rather —*behind* it. The president of the board caught up with me there."

Marcus's brow furrowed. "Caught up with you? Why?"

Soledad's jaw clenched. "He didn't appreciate the way I was allocating museum resources. He said I'd circumvented protocol. That I'd made payments to unvetted dealers and moved funds through unofficial channels."

Marcus stepped forward slightly, his tone sharpening. "Had you?"

She turned her full attention to him. "Yes. I had."

The air shifted. No spin. No denial. Just a clear, defiant truth.

"I was trying to recover pieces we'd lost—pieces scattered by colonizers, trafficked by opportunists, or carelessly sold to collectors who didn't know the meaning of what they owned. There was no time to wait for the board's blessing."

"And Curtis Vale?" I asked, my voice quieter. "Was he one of those opportunists?"

Soledad's nostrils flared—just once. "Vale was worse. He knew exactly what he was taking." She stormed off.

Soledad didn't walk far—just to the corner of the gallery, where a narrow wooden case displayed a curated selection of pre-Columbian jewelry. Her hand hovered over the glass but didn't touch it.

"I assume you want to know the rest," she murmured, her voice turned just slightly over her shoulder.

I nodded, though she wasn't looking. "Yes."

A quiet passed. Not silence—there was always the faint shuffle of custodians in the wings, the hum of the building itself—but it felt like the museum held its breath with us.

Soledad straightened. “I paid Gerardo Molina.”

I didn’t flinch. I just waited.

“Not because I trusted him,” she continued, finally turning back to face us. “He’s a scavenger. Opportunistic. But I thought…” Her hands folded together, knuckles white, “…I thought I could use him.”

Marcus’s voice was mild. “Use him how?”

“To recover what was lost.” Her tone dropped a register, slow and calculated. “Pieces scattered across borders. Forgotten. Exploited. The jaguar. Others. Our heritage—traded like trinkets, stashed in private vaults and auctioned off as décor.”

Her voice trembled then—just a twitch. But she reined it in.

“I’d filed paperwork. Tried official channels. But do you know how long it takes a federal claim to be processed? Years, if ever. And in that time, pieces vanish. Disappear into collections. Institutions. Personal hands that never open their doors.”

Marcus said nothing, just folded his arms and watched her.

Soledad stepped closer, her gaze direct. “He had contacts. Knew which dealers to approach, which shipments were coming in. He could trace leads no archivist could. I gave him money—quietly. Carefully. Always through intermediaries. It was a calculated risk.”

“But not legal,” I said.

“No,” she agreed. “But neither is what was done to us. Our national memory has been carved apart and sold to the highest bidder. You want to talk about crimes? Look in the display cases marked ‘Private Donation.’”

Her voice had taken on a sharp edge—passion burning through the veneer of academic poise. She was no longer just the museum's caretaker. She was its warrior. Its archivist. Its bleeding heart.

And that's when I realized how easy it would be to believe her.

And how dangerous that could be.

"So, you weren't trying to profit," Marcus said slowly. "You were trying to repatriate."

Soledad gave a bitter half-laugh. "I'm a scholar, Agent Evans. Do you know what we earn? I could barely afford the broker's fees, let alone a bribe large enough to rival Curtis Vale's offers. No, I was never going to beat him at that game. But I could try to intercept a few plays."

Marcus didn't move. But something about the way he shifted his weight, just slightly, told me he was tightening the screws.

"And you thought working with Molina would help?" he asked, his voice deceptively neutral.

Soledad didn't blink. Didn't flinch. Just held his gaze the way you'd hold a hot coal—steady, even if it burned a little.

"He was already part of the problem," she said. "I thought I could make him part of the solution."

Her tone was clipped but calm. No plea for understanding. No attempt to play the victim. Just a simple statement—one that could land in either court: strategy or desperation.

Marcus studied her a moment longer, then gave the smallest of nods, like he'd registered her answer but hadn't yet filed it under 'credible.'

I stepped in then—not to rescue her, but to reset the tone.

"Thank you for your honesty," I said.

Soledad turned to me, the corners of her mouth drawing into something that wasn't quite a smile and wasn't quite a threat.

"Don't mistake honesty for confession, Miss Finnegan."

"And the Navarro jaguar?" I asked quietly.

That stopped her. She didn't answer. Just looked at me with something almost pained in her expression.

"You know I've been trying," she said at last. "You've seen the plaque."

I nodded. *Pieza robada. En proceso de recuperación.*

"You were never going to let that label come down, were you?" I asked.

Soledad's voice was iron. "Not while the piece was still out there."

Marcus's eyes narrowed. "But you didn't get it back."

"No," she said softly. "Curtis beat me to it."

The moment held like a stretched string. Her motives made sense. Her methods, less so. If she'd crossed a line, was it in pursuit of justice—or revenge?

Sympathy warred with suspicion. And neither of them was winning.

Marcus's eyes narrowed. "And you were being chastised the night he died?"

"I was being dressed down like a schoolgirl," she said bitterly. "Behind a curtain of embroidered *tapetes*, with the sound of drums bleeding through the walls. He didn't want to risk a scene inside the museum. Too many donors. Too many ears."

"And you didn't leave your booth?" I asked.

"I wanted to," she said flatly. "I was furious. I needed air. But the confrontation dragged on. And by the time I broke away—"

She paused. Her mouth pressed flat. "Curtis Vale was already gone."

We stood in silence. The echo of the museum—normally reverent—now hummed with something colder. Sharper.

I exchanged a glance with Marcus. He looked thoughtful. Guarded.

Soledad folded her hands tightly in front of her, like she was trying to hide something. Guilt maybe?

"I was not the only one with something to lose," she added. "Don't forget that."

And with that, she turned back to the display, as if the winged jaguar that no longer stood there might yet offer some absolution.

As we turned to go, a thought tugged loose.

"You had a splinter," I mentioned, glancing back at Soledad. "The last time we were here. You said it was from handling old pieces."

Soledad gave a faint, rueful smile and held up the same hand. The skin had healed, but she rubbed the spot with her thumb, as though the memory had remained longer than the wound.

"It was from an old storage crate," she said. "Someone dropped off a bundle of carvings a few weeks ago, hoping we could help identify them. Some were genuine, some were tourist junk. They came packed in splintered pine and tied up with twine like a tamale. I wasn't careful."

She shrugged once, the corner of her mouth unmoving.

"I bled on a ledger page and got a tongue-lashing from the registrar," she added. "Occupational hazard."

Her tone was light. Brisk. But I caught the spark in Marcus's eyes. He wasn't thinking about the splinter itself—just the timing. Me, too.

We stepped out of the gallery and into the stone corridor, where sunlight slanted through arched windows and painted dust motes gold. Outside, the city was alive again—parade drums faint in the distance, a whiff of roasted corn already drifting in the breeze. But inside the museum, silence still clung like a second skin.

Marcus didn't speak.

He didn't have to—not at first. His jaw was relaxed, arms folded like they were keeping thoughts from spilling out. I could practically hear the wheels turning behind his diplomat's calm.

I gave him a few steps. Let the echo of our shoes fill the silence. Then, casually:

"Well?"

He stopped walking, turned to face the nearest column, and stared at it like it owed him an answer. Finally, he exhaled through his nose.

"She's either completely innocent," he said slowly, "or she's been playing the long game longer than anyone else."

He looked at me then—really looked at me. "And she's good, Darcy. If she's hiding something, it's buried deep."

I nodded once, more to myself than to him. Because I'd been thinking the same thing. There was something about Soledad that didn't rattle. Even under direct heat, she didn't melt—she tempered. Like steel. I turned toward the doors, letting the sun hit my face for the first time all morning.

Innocence or orchestration—either way, it was a game played in silence, not slip-ups. No fingerprints. Just fractures. And somewhere between the shadow and the story, we were still walking the fault line.

SMOKE AND MIRRORS

Marcus didn't say much as we walked, the sun shining over the bell towers. He walked a half step ahead, hands in his pockets, jaw tight in that way I'd come to recognize as mental triage. Whatever he was thinking, he wasn't ready to say it. Not yet.

Outside the museum, the city buzzed softly—less *comparsa* chaos, more murmur. The cobblestones were already warm from the sun, the air thick with a faint tang of mesquite smoke and roasted plantains. Someone played a slow *corrido* on a nylon-string guitar somewhere nearby, the notes curling into the air.

Marcus paused at the edge of the plaza. He didn't meet my gaze.

"I need to check in with HQ," he said finally, voice clipped. "Update them."

I nodded. "I'll catch up with Lizzie."

He nodded back. That was it. No awkward goodbye. No lingering glance. Just two people carrying too many questions in too little time. He sank onto the edge of a stone planter beneath the tree, already pulling out his phone. I let him.

I turned toward the square, scanning for the telltale bounce of curls and the undercurrent of chaos that came with traveling anywhere with Lizzie.

Sure enough, there she was at a nearby vendor's cart, arguing with a woman over the price of *alegrías*—a delicious Mexican sweet treat made of popped amaranth seeds and honey or *piloncillo,* unrefined cane sugar—like she was on the final round of a reality show called *The Great Oaxacan Haggle-Off.*

Mozart sat primly beside her, eyes locked on the pile of *alegrías* like he was preparing his closing argument.

"*Señora,*" Lizzie was saying earnestly, "I'm not saying they're not worth it. I'm saying you *want* me to tell all my American friends about these, don't you? That's marketing. What's that worth to you?"

The woman raised an eyebrow and, to her credit, didn't even blink.

Mozart sneezed, then looked at me as if to say, *Please rescue this woman before she barters away my dignity.*

I stepped up beside them.

"Been at it long?" I asked.

Lizzie turned, triumphant. "Long enough to earn us a buy-four-*alegrías*-get-one-free deal and a stern warning about chewing carefully."

The vendor passed her a little bundle wrapped in wax paper and tied with string. Lizzie grinned and pressed it to her chest like a sacred offering. Mozart got the first bite of the honeyed sweet treats.

I watched them, just for a second—my familiar little band that had become the only solid ground under my feet lately. My pulse had finally stopped hammering. My thoughts hadn't. But standing here, in the fading heat, watching Lizzie try to steal a second bite from a dog with faster reflexes, I realized how long it had been since I'd just… *exhaled.*

Behind me, the shadows of the museum stretched long across the plaza.

Soledad Pineda wasn't the only one hiding something. Gerardo Molina had been complicit in her backdoor dealings.

I need to find him and ask him about that suspicious looking chip in his red wooden cane.

We left the stall with the *alegrías,* a slightly offended vendor, and one very smug dog. Lizzie munched noisily beside me as we strolled through the quieter edge of the market, the sugar sticking to her fingers like glitter made from bees.

Mozart walked between us, nose low, tail swaying in a steady rhythm. The chaos of the parade had faded to a soft hum now—distant music, echoing laughter, the occasional pop of a leftover firecracker. Most of the vendor tents along this stretch were half-closed or being broken down altogether. Brightly painted *alebrijes* were wrapped in cloth. Tins of *chapulines*—toasted grasshoppers seasoned with chili, lime, garlic, and salt—were packed into crates. Lizzie wasn't even a little upset about that. Even the marigolds sagged a little now, their brilliant orange petals beginning to crisp at the edges like the festival itself had exhaled for the last time.

"It always feels like this after a big event," Lizzie said, as if reading my thoughts. "Like the magic's still here, but it's tired. Wants to go home and take its bra off." She tugged at her shirt. "I can relate."

I huffed a laugh, but it didn't quite reach the surface. My gaze swept the street—too quiet now, too orderly. No tourists shouting. No dancers spinning. Just the quiet rhythm of a city putting its mask back in the box.

"Everything's closing down," I murmured. "The market. The festival. Even our time here."

"You're not talking about the vendors."

"No," I said, low. "I'm talking about the list."

Lizzie crunched into the last bite of her *alegría* and brushed her hands together, sugar dust catching in the golden light. "You mean suspects."

"I mean everyone," I said. "Everyone who had a reason to want Curtis Vale dead. And everyone who's already lied about it."

I thought of Catalina's trembling fingers. Don Abel's haunted silence. Soledad's clipped deflections and that not-quite-denial about her time away from Oaxaca. I thought about the winged jaguar in the *mercado*—how it matched a carving that shouldn't exist anymore.

Mozart veered toward a lamppost, sniffed, decided against it, and returned to my heel like he had his own internal compass tuned to regret.

"I can feel it," I said. "We're close. Too close."

"To what?" Lizzie asked gently.

"That's the part that scares me," I said. "I'm not sure if it's the truth… or the next body."

She didn't answer right away. Just reached out and lightly touched my arm.

"You'll figure it out," she said. "You always do."

But for the first time since we landed in Oaxaca, I wasn't entirely sure that was true. Because something wasn't just wilting. Something was rotting underneath. And I was running out of time to dig it up.

As we wove past the quieter booths on the edge of the *mercado*, things seemed slower. I caught Lizzie up on what Soledad had revealed at the museum. She insisted on recapping Soledad's confession with the cadence of someone narrating a true crime podcast.

"So, let me get this straight," she said, adjusting her sunglasses like they were part of a press conference ensemble. "Vale double-crossed Molina. Molina got mad. But then you think Molina got back at him by working with Soledad. But Vale found out and got testy about the shoe being on the other foot. So, Vale confronts Molina. It gets physical. Vale got clumsy. Mezcal meets momentum, and bam—jaguar claw to the back?"

"It's possible."

Lizzie shrugged. "All I'm saying is, you've seen that cane. It could take a fellow out. One good shove, and—" She made a squelching sound with her mouth.

I had seen Molina's cane. And that splintered chip in the wood. In fact, I was watching it right now.

Across the plaza, in the shadow of a faded awning stitched with *papel picado* remnants, Gerardo Molina sat alone at a café table. A clay glass of something frothy—probably a *licuado*, that thick fruit-milk blend locals drank like Americans drank smoothies—rested beside him.

He looked older in the daylight. Less shadowy menace, more tired man with secrets he didn't want to repeat. But the alertness hadn't faded. His eyes moved constantly, scanning the space, never quite resting. He looked like a man used to being hunted—or worse, like one still deciding whether to run.

My gaze drifted to his cane, propped beside him against the metal chair leg. Reddish-orange. Navarro orange. The tip of it tapped occasionally against the concrete as if it, too, were impatient.

Lizzie followed my line of sight and smirked. "From *muy caliente* to the hot seat. You ready to question this guy?"

I didn't answer. Because as much as I'd once seen Molina as a threat, now... now he looked more like a cornered man than a killer. But sometimes, desperation makes for dangerous company.

Molina sat there—seated in the shade like someone determined not to melt. The tall *licuado* was so thick the straw stood straight without help. Papaya, maybe. Or mango. Something deceptively sunny for a man who looked like he hadn't smiled genuinely since the Cold War.

Lizzie peeled off with Mozart toward the *paleta* cart, waving two fingers without looking back. "Do you want lime or hibiscus?"

"Surprise me," I called, eyes already locked on my target.

I crossed the plaza alone.

Molina didn't acknowledge me until I was close enough to touch the chair across from him. His eyes shot up—dark, measuring. Not hostile. But not exactly friendly, either.

"Señor Molina," I said smoothly. "Do you mind?"

He gestured to the seat without a word.

I didn't waste time. "What was your arrangement with Curtis Vale?"

That got me a sigh. Deep. Tired. Like he'd hoped never to have this conversation but had rehearsed it all the same.

"You're direct," he said.

"I don't like small talk."

"Then I'll spare you mine," he said, adjusting the handkerchief he'd been dabbing across his brow. "Curtis Vale was a parasite. Polite. Charming. But underneath? Just another foreigner looking to make a buck off someone else's culture."

I frowned. "But isn't that what you do?"

"Depends upon your perspective, I suppose. I like to think of it as exposing the masses to my culture. But I never once claimed that the pieces I sold were originals. Just..."

"... homages," I finished.

He leaned back in his seat. "That's right. I foolishly

thought Vale was someone I could partner with. Go more global with my own operation."

"And your involvement?"

He snorted. "I introduced him to vendors. That's it. He had a tourist face. A clean accent. People trusted him. I told him who might be willing to sell knockoffs. Where the real artists were too proud—or too smart—to deal with him."

"No black-market trade in genuine artifacts? No smuggling ring?"

"If he built one, I wouldn't be invited," he said. "Curtis wanted cheap talent and plausible deniability. He didn't want a partner. He wanted a mask."

He tapped his cane once on the ground and looked past me, toward the marigold-strewn cobblestones.

"I gave him access," he said, low. "And he used it. That's all."

I watched him for a long moment. He didn't fidget. Didn't flinch. Just sat there, sweaty and grim, like a man who'd lost something he couldn't name.

And for the first time, I believed him. Or at least—I believed enough of him to know he wasn't the answer I'd been chasing.

Not anymore.

"Is that why you decided to work with Soledad Pineda? Because you found out about Vale's real game—making copies of lost and rare art and passing them off as the real thing?"

Molina shrugged. "I am a businessman. My job is to make money. But even I have my limits. So, when I saw that Vale had changed the terms of our arrangement, yes. Soledad Pineda approached me and promised me a hefty sum if I could help repatriate some of our lost heritage."

"And did your 'repatriation' methods include dispatching Curtis Vale to get the missing Navarro jaguar?"

Molina drew back, a puzzled frown pulling down the corners of his mouth. "You think I killed Vale?"

He broke out in a hearty belly laugh. The sound drew Mozart's attention. He broke free of Lizzie's grip on his leash and ran back toward me, ready to defend me if necessary.

"Mozzie!" Lizzie called.

I reached down and grabbed Mozart's collar as he growled at Molina.

"Mozzie!" I scolded half-heartedly. Secretly, I was a little glad for his presence.

Lizzie abandoned the popsicle cart and rushed over. She eyed Molina suspiciously. "Is everything okay over here?"

Molina wiped a tear from his eye. "*Si, si.* It's just your friend here who thinks I sent Señor Vale to join the legions of *Dia de los Muertos*."

"Did you?" Lizzie asked, point blank.

Molina leveled a stare at her. "Vale was a young man. I am old. I walk with a cane." He grabbed the cane from its resting place.

The motion made me start. Mozzie growled again, low and threatening.

"Still," I began, "that cane would make an awfully convenient weapon. Even an older man, such as yourself, could use it as leverage to gain an advantage over someone of Mr. Vale's age." I pointed. "Is that how it got that chip? Did the two of you fight?"

Molina's eyes drifted to the chip in the russet-colored wood. "This?" He rubbed his finger over the spot. "No. Your Senor Mozart is not the only *perrito* in Oaxaca. I was visiting my daughter. My little granddaughter has a chihuahua who likes to chew."

Mozart stopped growling. He took a tentative step toward Molina and cautiously sniffed his cane near the scarred spot. He snorted and snuffed, a sequence of sounds he usually only made when he smelled another dog. And I trusted Mozzie's instincts.

Didn't mean I was ready to trust Molina. Not just yet.

"Okay," I agreed. "But can you tell me where you were at the time of Vale's death? I know you were at the *mercado*."

Molina shook his head. "I had only just arrived when Vale's body was discovered. I was out near Santa María del Tule—picking up a set of carved tapetes from a widow who doesn't sell through official channels. She's old-school. Won't ship. Won't register. I was doing what I've always done—finding beauty before it disappears."

Mozart let out an agreeable bark. He looked up at me with those soulful eyes of his. He trotted over to Molina, who rewarded him with a hearty rub and a stray piece of *churro* from the plate next to his drink.

"You can ask her," Molina continued. "Or the bus driver. I hitched a ride back in his empty shuttle van once I realized how late it had gotten. You think I'd risk that deal just to pick a fight with a drunk foreigner in a plaza full of cameras?" He pointed to the small, subtle cameras under the eaves of several of the nearby buildings.

"Cameras," Lizzie groaned. "Of course!"

I gave myself a mental facepalm, too. I was so enamored of Oaxacan tradition and the historical aspect of the place, I had not assumed there would be modern security. I chastised myself for the assumption.

"I actually recommended them. Can't be too careful. Hard to know who to trust, really." A sly smile crooked the corners of his lips. "We haven't had them for long—only a year or two—but they are there. If you weren't a regular in the *mercado*, you might not even know they were there, even if you lived here. Now, if you will excuse me." He pulled himself to his feet. "I am going to spend the last day of Dia de los Muertos with my family."

Molina limped away on his cane, still managing to look regal. Lizzie slumped into his abandoned seat.

"Cameras. Why didn't we think of that?" she mumbled.

"I'm sure the police did," I answered.

"Not if they thought it was just some 'tragic accident.' Everybody's been so caught up in the festival, it seemed they were happy enough to sweep it under the rug," she stated. She wasn't wrong.

Only a year or two. So, someone like Soledad might not know they were there. But then, I had gotten the impression that Don Abel didn't often venture into the *mercado*. It was possible he was unaware of their existence, too. I couldn't imagine Catalina, with her stall in the *mercado*, would not be aware of them.

The question gnawed at my brain.

"You think the cameras caught Vale's killer on tape?" Lizzie asked.

"Let's hope so, because the festival is almost over." The squeaky wheel of a moving cart sounded behind us as the vendor wheeled it away.

"Maybe Marcus can get us access to the videos. What do you say? Are you, ready to nab a killer?" I asked, jumping to my feet. Mozart bounced on all fours, like he was excited to join in the chase.

"Sure," Lizzie groaned as she reluctantly stood. "But I'd rather be shopping."

THE FOOTAGE AND THE FALL

Mozart had just finished nibbling the last crumb of *churro* Lizzie had slipped him from Molina's abandoned plate when Marcus reappeared—no fanfare, no rush, just that steady, deliberate walk that told me whatever Interpol had said hadn't lightened his mood.

He paused at the edge of the market stall, one hand in his pocket, the other running absently over the back of his neck. His shirt sleeves were still rolled, but the collar was newly wrinkled, like he'd been tugging at it the whole walk back.

Lizzie looked up from her price haggling and gave him a cheery wave. "Tell me you're here for snacks and not doom."

He didn't smile.

"Interpol agrees," he said, voice low enough to disappear into the chatter of the *mercado*. "What Molina was doing for Soledad—it's shady—but there's not enough to charge him."

I wiped a smudge of cinnamon off my wrist and nodded. "Good. I already let him go."

That got a reaction. A blink. A slow exhale through the nose.

"So," he said, almost smiling. "You're ahead of me now."

"Wasn't I always?"

"You're dangerous."

Lizzie let out a snort. Mozart gave a soft approving whuff, as if solving transnational crimes without jurisdiction was just another Tuesday.

Marcus didn't rise to the bait. He looked tired—not just physically, but somewhere deeper. Like his certainty had finally met its match and hadn't come out clean. His silence said more than his words. And we were only just getting started.

We started walking—nowhere in particular, just following the scent of roasted corn and the tail end of the crowd.

Marcus didn't say anything for a bit. I didn't push. Lizzie fell behind to coo over a *papel picado* vendor who had somehow worked a dog's face—one that looked remarkably like Mozart—into a sugar skull design in the flag, and I was half-listening to her when something clicked in my brain.

"You know," I said, keeping my tone light, "Molina mentioned something interesting."

Marcus looked over, brows raised in mild alarm.

"Relax," I said. "He said the *mercado* has cameras."

Marcus stopped walking.

"You didn't know?"

He didn't answer right away. Just stared toward the cluster of rooftops beyond the plaza like he was rechecking every memory he had of the crime scene.

"I missed them," he said finally, quietly.

I gave him a look. "You?"

He smiled, but it didn't reach his eyes. "That's what I mean."

"Mean what?"

He glanced at me, a slow half-turn, and his voice dropped just enough to register as something that might've once been a secret. "You are inherently more dangerous than the criminals I chase."

I blinked. "Why?"

Marcus looked straight ahead again. "Because when you're around… I can't see anything else."

The words landed somewhere between my sternum and my last good sense. I said nothing.

But I felt everything.

And for the briefest second, the world blurred—winged jaguar carvings, *mezcal* schemes, stolen artifacts—all softening into something I wasn't ready to name.

Behind us, Lizzie let out a dreamy sigh loud enough to draw stares from three *papel picado* skeletons and a *churro* vendor.

"Please tell me someone got that on tape," she whispered. "I'd like to replay it at your wedding."

I shot her a look, but she was already fanning herself with a festival program and giving Mozart a conspiratorial pat on the head like he was her emotional support witness.

Marcus, to his credit, pretended not to hear. Which made me like him more. And hate myself, just a little.

Because Lizzie was wrong.

That moment wasn't romantic.

It was distracting.

And distractions were dangerous.

Especially the kind that walked beside you with a five o'clock shadow and a file full of Interpol credentials.

I turned away, letting the festival swirl around us again—colors and noise and the slow descent of the last marigold petals drifting like golden punctuation.

Had I really pulled his focus?

Had I gotten so caught up in my own sleuthing spiral that I'd become a liability?

I shook it off. I didn't have time for melodrama or misplaced feelings. Not now.

Curtis Vale was still dead. His killer is still out there. And someone had used this festival—this celebration of life and memory—to bury the truth.

I chastised myself. No more missed clues. No more blurred lines. It was time to see clearly. Everything. And everyone.

We made our way across the plaza to a narrow storefront wedged between a *dulcería* and a shop that seemed to sell nothing but embroidered tortilla warmers. A small hand-painted sign above the door read *"Artesanía y Audio Visuales"*, which, given the tangle of security cables and alebrije keychains in the window, seemed just ambiguous enough to be promising.

Inside, it smelled like dust, floor wax, and tamarind gum. The clerk—a man in his fifties with meticulous hair and the wariness of someone who'd been burned by tourists before—looked up from a ledger with a frown that barely wavered at our entrance.

Marcus stepped forward, calm and crisp. No badge-flash theatrics. Just a smooth reach into his inner jacket pocket and a quiet, "Interpol. We're hoping you can help."

That got the man's attention.

His gaze darted to me, then Lizzie, then Mozart—who was currently trying to decide whether the basket of pom-pom keychains by the door was edible or merely decorative.

"We're hoping to view footage from the Day of the Dead festival," Marcus continued. "Specifically the plaza and the jaguar sculpture on the west end."

The man blinked, once. Then motioned toward the back without a word.

We followed him past a curtain of glass beads into a narrow office that held a humming monitor, a tangle of cords, and an old oscillating fan that turned just slow enough to be judgmental.

"Gracias," I said, as he began scrubbing through the footage.

Mozart flopped down with an exaggerated groan, his paws splayed like he'd been forced to run a marathon instead of wandering past three *churro* carts and a man juggling coconuts.

Lizzie leaned close and whispered, "My money's on María. Or Catalina. No, wait... Don Abel in disguise."

I didn't respond. I was watching the screen as the timestamp crept forward.

If the truth was in that feed, we were about to see it. Ready or not.

The footage was chaotic. A riot of color and motion. Confetti spiraled like paper rain. Costumed skeletons twirled past the edge of the frame. A float shaped like a flaming rooster blazed across the screen and promptly blocked the view of the jaguar sculpture with a dramatic puff of smoke.

"Helpful," I muttered.

Marcus leaned closer, one hand braced on the table, his jaw tight. Lizzie leaned on the other side, popcorn-less but narrating like this was her favorite *telenovela*.

Mozart stayed sprawled on the tile like the only adult in the room.

After another minute of festival fanfare, the screen shifted. There—barely visible in the bottom left corner—was the base of the jaguar sculpture. The tip of one claw just peeked into frame, barely more than a shadow against the mosaic stone.

Just beyond it: crates. Wooden, weather-worn. Stacked two high with a paper banner draped lazily over them—probably part of the installation, or a lazy attempt at decor. They looked unremarkable.

Until Curtis Vale appeared.

He came into view from the far right, striding like he owned the square. He was wearing the same jacket he'd been found in. I felt my stomach tighten.

He walked straight toward the crates, scanned the crowd, and then placed something long and paper-wrapped across the top. He adjusted it. Nudged it like it mattered. The paper was brown. Wrinkled. Familiar.

"That's it," I said. "That's the package María had at the airport."

Marcus nodded silently.

Curtis stepped back. He took out his phone. Looked around.

And then—María.

She entered the frame from the crowd, shoulders stiff, lips moving fast. Her hair was pulled back tight, her face flushed. She went right for the crate. Pointed at the bundle.

Curtis responded—smirking, gesturing. Whatever they were saying, it wasn't cordial. She snatched the package. Her hands tore through the paper with a kind of desperate fury—like she was peeling away a lie. The paper crinkled, unfurled, and fell open.

I leaned forward.

Inside was the jaguar carving.

Catalina's carving. Unmistakable in its resemblance. The spiraled eye. The snarl that wasn't quite feral but not friendly either. The vivid Navarro orange and fuchsia swirling across the snout like it had been kissed by fire.

María stared at it. And then her whole body went taut. Not with fear. With recognition. With rage.

She turned to Curtis, jabbing a finger first at the carving, then toward the jaguar sculpture—barely in frame behind the crates. Her mouth moved. No sound, but we could read it in her face. In the set of her jaw. In the sharp cut of her gestures.

Curtis stepped toward her, fast and full of bluster. That smug swagger we'd heard so much about rearing up like a snake. María didn't back away. She shoved him. Hard. Curtis staggered. Off-balance. Out of frame.

The crowd turned. All at once.

Heads pivoted. Mouths fell open in silent gasps. Hands covered frightened eyes. Then the camera jostled as someone bumped the table it sat on. But before the angle shifted entirely, I saw it.

The very tip of the jaguar sculpture's claw—stained with red.

Maria's face didn't register triumph. It registered terror. Her hands hovered at her mouth like she wasn't sure whether to cover a scream or force one out. She stared at where Curtis had vanished—eyes wide, stunned. Frozen in place for three long seconds.

And then… she moved.

Not wildly. Not frantically. Just—moved. Smoothly. Quietly. Like she'd trained for this exact moment. She stepped back, adjusted the scarf around her shoulders, and turned into the stream of celebrants.

In less than ten seconds, she was gone.

One of the dancing devils bumped the crates a moment later. A child darted across the screen chasing a spinning noisemaker. A balloon floated up. María had melted into the crowd like a ghost.

Behind me, Lizzie let out a shaky breath. "So… María killed him?"

Marcus didn't take his eyes off the screen. "Looks that way."

His voice wasn't cold. Just certain. Final.

But I couldn't shake the look on María's face—right

before she vanished. It hadn't been cold-blooded. It had been something else.

The footage paused—Marcus's finger hovering over the keyboard as the camera caught just the edge of the jaguar sculpture in the frame. Not the full thing. Just one outstretched claw, jagged and painted in that unmistakable Navarro *naranja*, its edges chipped, one splinter practically glowing under the overhead light.

"There," I said, pointing.

Marcus leaned in. "That carving splintered when Vale hit it."

Lizzie let out a slow exhale. "The splinter. In Maria's sleeve. We brushed it off."

I remembered it now. The tiny shard snagged in the fabric at the graveyard. The bit of red-orange wood that had gotten wedged in Mozart's paw. My eyes widened. I frantically patted the pockets of my jeans. Yes, I had worn them for three days on this trip. Don't judge. I blame the high cost of checked baggage.

Yes! It was still there. I fished out the piece of wood. Not just a stray splinter anymore.

Evidence.

A breath I didn't realize I was holding escaped through my nose. "No one even noticed. Confetti was falling. Music was blasting. It was a parade of sensory overload."

Marcus nodded. "And she walked away with a sliver of the murder weapon stuck to her."

"Yeesh," Lizzie said, wrapping her arms around herself. "Killer confetti. I don't like it."

Neither did I.

I stared at the screen, at the jagged moment frozen in digital memory.

"That doesn't add up," I said slowly. "Didn't we already

establish that Catalina was Curtis's carver? Even if she didn't know it at the time?"

"Yes," Lizzie said, still perched on the edge of the desk like a crime-scene commentator. "Catalina made the piece. The winged jaguar. Which means Vale didn't need a pickup. So, that blows a hole in the theory that he was meeting Maria at the airport for a handoff."

I leaned back in the chair, rubbing my temple. "Maybe he really did steal it from her that day. Just grabbed the package and took off."

"Right," Lizzie said, pointing at the screen again. "But if that package was hers—if it came from her hands—why did she look so surprised when she opened it?"

We watched her expression again. Frame by frame. Shock. Not fear. Not anger. Recognition. Wrongness.

Marcus drew his arms across his chest, eyes narrowing. "You think Vale swapped it?"

"Maybe," I said. "Or maybe María knew—without a doubt—that the jaguar in *that* package wasn't what it was supposed to be."

A long pause stretched out between us. Mozart let out a low whine, as if even he could sense we were entering a darker tunnel.

"So," Lizzie said softly. "What does that mean?"

I stared at Maria's frozen expression. "It means we just unlocked a new mystery."

And for the first time all day, I didn't have a single theory ready to explain it.

THE COLOR THAT STAYED

I was supposed to be packing. Instead, I was pacing.

Casa de las Bugambilias glowed in the late afternoon light, the golden hour casting warm fingers across the courtyard tiles and creeping through the open shutters of our room. Outside, the scent of bougainvillea tangled with cinnamon and woodsmoke, and in another life, maybe I would have been writing a food column about just that.

But not today.

Maria had vanished—not just into the crowd, but from the hotel entirely. Her room was still registered. Her keycard hadn't been turned in. But according to the *señora* at the front desk, she hadn't been seen since the *comparsa*. Gone. Evaporated. Like the end of a dream you couldn't quite remember.

Marcus had gone to file an official report with his headquarters, frustration written in every line of his posture. He hadn't said as much, but I could tell he felt he'd let her slip through the cracks. And that bothered him more than he wanted to admit.

Lizzie, meanwhile, was painting her toenails.

"I can't go home with ugly feet," she said, sprawled across her bed with a towel under one leg and a bottle of polish clutched between two fingers. "There might be a cute guy on the plane."

"You haven't packed a single thing," I replied, nudging her discarded suitcase with my foot.

She fluttered her free hand like a bored flamenco dancer. "Packing's easy. Emotional closure is harder."

I shook my head and turned toward the dresser. "You've been watching too many *telenovelas*."

"Better than rewatching the footage of a murder on loop in my head."

Fair point.

Mozzie, curled at the foot of her bed, lifted his head and gave a small whine. I lobbed a rolled-up sock toward the suitcase. He thought it was a toy, sprang up, and immediately barreled straight into Lizzie's outstretched foot.

The nail polish bottle tipped, teetered, and then—

"Oh no, no, no—"

Too late.

Red-orange lacquer pooled onto Lizzie's white linen pants in a bloom that spread like wildfire.

"Seriously?" she groaned, scrambling to blot the stain.

I grabbed the towel from under her leg and tried to dab the mess. "It looks like a crime scene."

She held up her pant leg, scowling. "Navarro *naranja*," she muttered. "Great. Now it's haunting me, too."

But my hands stilled.

Navarro *naranja*.

The color on Maria's jacket. A shade only people in the family knew how to make. And then it hit me. "What if she knew?"

Lizzie blinked. "Knew what?"

"What if Maria didn't just recognize the carving because

it was Catalina's work. What if she recognized it… because she'd carved the original?"

Her eyes widened. "Wait. Are you saying Maria is…?"

"Lucia." I said it aloud. And the name settled in the air like a truth. "The daughter Don Abel thought died in the fire."

Lizzie sat up straighter, mouth slightly open. "But that means…"

"She didn't die. She disappeared. And if she's the one who carved the original Navarro jaguar… then, of course, she'd know the one in that package wasn't the original. Of course she'd be furious. That wasn't just a betrayal of her family. It was a desecration of her identity."

Mozzie gave a sharp bark, as if punctuating the moment.

I turned toward the door.

Lizzie didn't have to ask. She just nodded and capped the polish.

"I think," I said, "it's time we ask Don Abel a very difficult question."

* * *

Don Abel opened the door before we knocked. Not surprised. Not impatient. Just… braced.

"You've returned," he said.

"We need to ask you something," I said.

He held the door, and the silence stretched long enough for the wood to creak in protest.

Inside, the house hadn't changed. The altar still flickered in the corner. The unfinished jaguar still waited beneath its drop cloth. And Don Abel still moved like a man whose life had been carved down to the grain.

He gestured for us to sit.

We didn't.

I took a breath. "You told me your daughter died in the fire."

His face didn't change. Not at first. But something behind his eyes stilled—like water before a storm.

"She did," he said. Quiet. Certain.

Lizzie and Mozzie stood behind me, silent.

"I need to ask you something difficult," I said. "Please hear it all the way through."

He nodded once, though I could already see his jaw tighten.

"There's a woman," I said. "She's been in the market. Quiet. Watchful. She called herself María."

His brow furrowed, but he didn't speak.

"She has a way with children. A calm that's almost practiced."

"She was always good with Catalina," Don Abel admitted.

I nodded solemnly. "And she wears her pain like a jacket that never comes off." I paused. "She also had a streak of paint on her shoulder. Navarro *naranja*."

That got him. The barest flinch.

"I've seen her carving," I said. "She's good. Too good."

His hand twitched at his side, curling slightly over the scarred fingers of his left hand.

"She was there the day Curtis Vale died," I said softly. "She argued with him. She left before the crowd scattered. She knew him. She had a wrapped parcel the day he arrived. He stole it from her. He had it there with him at the *mercado*. Or so she thought. But when she opened it… she looked surprised. Furious. Betrayed."

His voice came low. Ragged. "What are you saying?"

"I'm saying…" I swallowed. "What if the girl you carried out of the fire wasn't Lucia?"

The silence wasn't loud. It was hollow.

A void. A space being carved out in real time.

"I buried her," he whispered.

"No," I said gently. "You buried someone. And you believed it was her."

His eyes met mine. And I watched the impossible bloom there.

"No one questioned it," he said. "The flames… there wasn't much. But she was in the workshop that night. I saw her go in."

"But what if she got out?" I asked. "What if she ran—and didn't come back?"

He shook his head once. But it wasn't denial.

It was disbelief unspooling.

"She loved to run," he murmured, almost to himself. "Even when she was small. Always fast. Always out of reach."

"She could've changed her name," I said. "Taken the blame. The shame. The weight of all of it—and just… disappeared."

He stared at me. "You think this María… is my daughter?"

"I don't know for certain," I said. "But I think you might."

Don Abel's shoulders dropped—not slumped, but released, like he was letting go of something he hadn't known he was still holding.

"If it is her," he said hoarsely, "why wouldn't she come back?"

"Maybe she thought she couldn't."

He looked at the altar, then at the jaguar beneath the cloth. "Then I failed her twice."

"No," I said. "You loved her enough to remember. That's why we're here."

He didn't cry.

But I saw something loosen in his face—like a knot untying just enough to let the truth begin to breathe.

He looked like a man hollowed out from the inside—like

something ancient and sorrowing had finally cracked just enough to let the air in.

I didn't move or speak. Not until a soft creak sounded behind me.

Catalina stood in the doorway, eyes wide, arms folded like she was physically holding herself together. I had no idea how long she'd been there.

Long enough.

"You think my sister is alive?" Her voice was barely above a whisper. "And that she killed Curtis?"

Don Abel's expression shifted in an instant—pain curling into something darker at the mention of Vale's name.

"I don't think it was intentional," I said gently. "She shoved him. That part's clear. But he'd been drinking. He wasn't steady. The square was chaotic. A stumble, a jagged claw, a festival crowd… it was the perfect storm."

Don Abel dropped his head into his hands.

Catalina stepped into the room. Slowly. Like the air was too thick to breathe. She crossed to her father, crouched beside him, and placed one hand lightly over his scarred knuckles.

"I never thought…" she began, then trailed off. "All these years, I thought I was the one who disappointed you."

He didn't look up. But his fingers curled around hers.

Catalina's gaze turned to me. "Where is she now?"

"We don't know," I admitted. "After what happened… she vanished. Left the hotel. Didn't return to her room. No one's seen her since."

"If she really is your sister," Lizzie added softly, "it might be a secret she takes with her to the grave."

Catalina looked like she'd been slapped with silence.

She stood slowly, her brow furrowed, lips pressing together in thought.

"When we were little," she said quietly, "Lucía used to tell me that if she ever had a secret—one too big for words—she'd hide it where no one looks."

She turned to face me fully now. "She said she'd hide it in the sky."

I blinked. "That's... poetic. But what does that mean?"

Don Abel's head rose. "Hierve el Agua."

Catalina nodded.

I squinted. "The water boils?"

Don Abel gave a small, wry smile—though the grief hadn't left his eyes. "Yes. But that's not what it means to us."

He rose stiffly, moving toward the window. The light hit the altar just right, making the candle glow as if it were newly lit.

"Before the fire... before the loss... we used to take walks as a family. Up above the falls. My wife called it 'walking above the gods.'"

"The sky," I echoed, feeling the goosebumps rise on my arms.

Catalina's voice was steadier now. "It's quiet there. Still. She always said that if she needed to remember who she was, she'd go there."

Don Abel nodded, eyes distant. I reached for my phone. Scrolled quickly. I found Marcus's contact and pressed the call.

"She won't be hiding in a crowd this time," I stated. "She'll be where no one looks."

My thumb hovered for a beat before I hit send.

I think I know exactly where Lucía Navarro is.

RETURN TO THE EDGE

By the time we reached the trailhead, the morning heat was already tugging at my shirt. The climb to *Hierve el Agua* wasn't steep, exactly, but it made you feel every bad decision you'd ever made—especially if you were dragging the weight of unfinished questions behind you.

Marcus walked beside me, silent as ever when he had too much on his mind. I had to explain to him how I knew that the woman claiming to be María was really Lucía Navarro.

Mozart trotted just ahead, nose twitching at the air, tail high but alert.

The limestone cliffs shimmered with that eerie illusion of water—like petrified waterfalls frozen mid-cascade, cascading down from rock that held secrets too old to speak. Nature here wasn't still. It just waited.

At the summit, just past a tangle of low brush, we saw her.

Lucía.

She stood alone at the ledge, her back to us, arms wrapped loosely around her torso as if holding herself together was an hourly task. No jacket this time—just a sleeveless cotton tank that clung to her back in the sun. That's when I saw them. Faint, but unmistakable. Scars. Long and pale, faded like grief that had tried to heal but never fully let go.

She turned when she heard us. And she didn't run.

"I hoped someone would come," she said softly.. "So someone could carry my apology to my father."

My throat closed. "You're Lucía Navarro."

She nodded.

"You escaped the fire."

She looked down at her scars. "I don't think I will ever truly escape the fire."

Behind us, stones scraped. I turned in time to see Don Abel emerge from the trail, Lizzie and Catalina hovering anxiously a few steps behind him.

"You brought them?" I whispered.

Lizzie shrugged, eyes wide. "They needed to come. They deserve the truth too."

Don Abel didn't shout. Didn't lurch. He just stood there, taking her in like a man who'd seen a ghost and didn't know whether to fall to his knees or turn to salt.

Lucía's shoulders hunched.

"I didn't mean to leave," she said. "I was trying to stay warm. We lit a small fire... just a little one. My friend—a girl named Marielena, sixteen, like me—she said no one would care."

Her voice cracked.

"But I was stupid. I left the turpentine too close. The fire jumped. We were surrounded so fast."

She pressed a hand to her ribs.

"She got trapped. I tried—I swear, I tried—but..."

Her voice dissolved into the wind. Even Mozart stood frozen, ears tipped forward like he understood.

"I panicked," she whispered. "I ran. All I could grab was

the jaguar. The sacred one. I thought... if I could save just that..."

"You let us believe you died," Don Abel said. Not angry. Just broken.

"I couldn't face what I'd done. I hid in an old abandoned shack on the outskirts of town. And later, when I dared come close enough into town to steal food or water, I heard the stories... that the winged jaguar had perished too, I knew I'd made things worse. But I kept it hidden. I protected it."

She looked up at him.

"After Mamá died, I decided to come back. I thought maybe... maybe it was time."

Don Abel stared at her. "You were alive. And you had the jaguar? All this time?"

"Yes."

His voice cracked. "I thought I lost both you and the jaguar that night."

"But what part did Curtis Vale play in all this?" Marcus asked, edging warily closer to Lucía.

"I had met Curtis in Texas. I was working for an art dealer in Dallas when he came in one day to speak with my boss. He said he had some Oaxacan art to sell. Would he be interested? My boss passed on the idea, but I was interested. It was the first breath of home I'd had since I left."

She looked sadly at her father and sister.

"He invited me to lunch to look at the pieces and discuss the art. I told him the pieces he had were crude examples of the craft. I didn't recognize any of the styles, but then I hadn't been home for a long time. I told him I came from a family of carvers. I didn't mention the name. I didn't dare."

She wrung her hands together. I noticed Don Abel was mirroring her, wringing his own scarred hands together.

"I knew I shouldn't," Lucía continued, "but I had not been able to discuss my art with anyone forever. I asked him if he wanted to see *real* Oaxacan art. We arranged to meet again, and I showed him the winged jaguar. His eyes sparkled, which gave me great joy. He particularly loved the colors and the signature swirl. He asked me how much I wanted for it. I had to tell him it was not for sale. He gave me his card. Told me if I ever changed my mind, or was going to Oaxaca, to give him a call."

She stepped forward. "I didn't hear from him again. Not until Mamá died. Curtis Vale had figured out who I was. I had no idea it was because he had been using Catalina—seen her designs—the one that so closely mimicked my own. He called me at the art dealers. Said not to worry, my secret was safe with him, but he had learned my mother had passed. Many said of grief. He said it was time I came home. To bring me and the jaguar and give the family closure. He said he would meet me at the airport."

She stared over the falls. "You know the rest."

"That's when he stole the jaguar," I murmured.

She nodded. "He knew right where I was going to be and what I was going to have with me."

"What happened the night Vale died?" Marcus asked, quietly.

Lucía looked away. "We argued. He grabbed my arm. Tried to take the carving. I shoved him. He tripped. The jaguar—" She swallowed. "It was an accident."

Silence spread like water over stone.

"I didn't mean to kill him," she said.

We believed her. But belief, like memory, wasn't always enough to save you.

Catalina, who had been silent as stone until now, moved beside her sister. "She saved it, Papa. All this time. She kept the jaguar safe."

Don Abel's eyes were glassy. He turned to Catalina. "You were right. The jaguar is still watching over our family."

He reached a shaking hand to Lucía's face. "It has kept your sister safe for us all this time."

Lucía broke, sagging into his arms.

"But, Papa," she wept. "I've done terrible things. I've lost our sacred family totem. Who knows where Vale has sent it?"

Don Abel drew up a little taller, his voice forging steel from sorrow. He looked down at Catalina's stomach—at the promise of what came next.

"Our family… it may be broken… but we are Navarros. We are strong. We must… carve out a new life. I realize that now."

Don Abel turned to Marcus. "What will happen to my daughter? She will go to jail?"

Marcus's voice was measured, but not without empathy. "Possibly. She'll have to answer for what happened. But once the local authorities see the footage—see that Vale attacked her first—they may be lenient."

Lucía met his gaze. "I'll do whatever it takes. Just… no more lies."

The family embraced—three broken pieces finding one another again. But emotion is a fragile floor. As Catalina stepped back, her foot skidded on the damp stone edge slick from mineral spray. She slipped—hands flailing—

"Cata!" Lucía screamed.

Marcus lunged forward—

—but it was Lucía who caught her, gripping her wrist with a strength born of guilt and blood and something ancestral.

The strength of the jaguar.

"I've got you," she whispered.

"I was not worried." Catalina forced a smile as she clung to her sister's arm. "I knew the jaguar was watching."

Marcus reached forward, gripping Catalina's arms along with Lucía. They pulled her back together. Don Abel dropped to one knee, his palm pressed to the rock like he was thanking the mountain itself.

Mozart barked once, tail thumping, then trotted over to Lucía, laying his head gently on her foot.

Lizzie exhaled hard. "So. Just a normal day in Oaxaca."

I didn't answer. I was watching Lucía.

Her face had changed—not lighter. Not unburdened. But somehow... truer.

She had been forged in fire. But this was where she was finally allowed to cool.

The End.

EPILOGUE

Epilogue – A Dance with the Living

The bags were packed. Mozart's collar had been demarigolded—by mutual agreement. And the sky above Oaxaca blazed with the last fire-kissed hues of *Día de los Muertos,* like it knew the festival was ready to surrender itself back to memory.

It was the final night. Not just of the holiday—but of something else I couldn't quite name. Closure, maybe. Or the kind of peace you only earned after walking headfirst into someone else's sorrow and making it out with both empathy and evidence intact.

The plaza was alive again—not with fear, but with celebration. Candles glimmered from every *ofrenda. Papel picado* snapped in the breeze like applause. Brass music swelled beneath the glowing paper lanterns that hung in neat rows overhead.

And there, in the middle of it all, Marcus held out his hand. No words. Just a look.

I took it.

We danced slowly, our feet shuffling over warm cobblestone, his hand at the small of my back, Mozart curled nearby on a cushion one of the *abuelas* had declared "sacred *perrito* ground." The music wasn't fast, but neither were we. It was the kind of dance you shared after surviving something together. Or before you said goodbye.

We swayed past the main fountain—its base ringed in marigolds and glittering votives—and that's when we saw them. Soledad and Molina. Dancing. Together.

Her blouse was embroidered in indigo and gold. His cane was leaned casually against a nearby wall. Still, he seemed to float across the dance floor without it. The way she looked at him—steadily, like the answer to a very old question—told me more than any confession ever could.

Soledad broke away to greet us, eyes sparkling.

"Have you heard the news?" she asked.

Marcus and I glanced at each other, both shaking our heads.

Molina stepped forward, looking proud enough to light up the *zócalo* all by himself. "We've recovered it."

"The winged jaguar?" I asked.

Soledad nodded. "The original Navarro carving. It was in a storage unit Vale rented under a shell name outside Puebla. Gerardo used his contacts to track it down."

Marcus blinked. "You're kidding."

"Not even a little," Soledad said.

"Don't suppose you've ever considered a second career in Interpol, have you?" Marcus asked Molina.

The older man laughed. "I think no. Too many rules."

"The Navarro *yaguar* is already on its way home," Soledad chuckled.

"To the Navarros?" I asked, glancing around instinctively for Don Abel or Catalina.

"They've agreed to let the museum house it," Soledad replied. "Don Abel said… 'Strength should be shared.'"

My breath caught for a second.

Marcus slipped his hand back into mine. "Looks like we're not the only ones dancing with history."

Before I could answer, a familiar voice rang out.

"Oh, well isn't this just painfully romantic." Lizzie strolled up, Mozart trotting beside her in full festive fluff. He had abandoned his pillow to investigate what Lizzie held in her hand. I think he was hoping for a *churro*.

Lizzie sized Molina and Soledad up and down. "I said it before and I'll say it again, Señor Molina. *Muy caliente*."

They laughed and spun off into the crowd.

Lizzie turned back to me. Mozart kept jumping up, trying to sniff what she was holding. It was small and wrapped in tissue paper. "For you," she said, handing it to me.

I unwrapped it slowly. It was a tiny, hand-carved figurine. Mozart—clearly modeled off my favorite fuzzy guy—with the curled tail of a jaguar.

"Schnoodle jaguar," she said with pride. "Or, as I like to call it, the Mozaguar."

Mozart immediately sneezed on it.

Lizzie smirked. "Critic."

I pocketed it anyway.

"Ah, well," she said. "What do you think, Mozzie? One last *churro?*"

He looked at her with such adoration it could only be interpreted as, *You had me at churro.*

The music shifted to a slow ballad played on violins and *guitarróns,* warm and golden.

Marcus leaned in. "I'm leaving in the morning."

"I figured."

He hesitated. "And you? What's next? Still headed home?"

"Eventually. I have a few weeks in New York first, but

then it's Thanksgiving," I shrugged. "My mother can't do it without my cranberry relish this year."

He smiled. "Sounds... tart."

"It is," I said. "Also oddly beloved."

There was a beat. Then, like it had just occurred to me, I added, "You should come."

His eyes widened. "To Thanksgiving?"

I nodded. "At the Finnegans'."

His mouth opened. Closed. Reopened. "And... meet your family?"

Behind us, Lizzie dropped her *churro*. Mozart was only too happy to pick it up.

"Ohhhhhhh," Lizzie said dramatically. "This is gonna be good."

Mozzie barked once, and I swear even he looked surprised.

And just like that—amid the laughter, the shimmering candlelight, and the slow shuffle of our feet—I realized something.

Dia de los Muertos wasn't just about remembering the dead. It was about choosing to live.

And this time, I was walking home with more than answers. I was walking home with possibility.

Thank you for reading my latest adventures. I truly appreciate your support and need your help with an Amazon review.

Please Click to leave your review.

If you enjoyed reading ***Murder, Marigolds & Mezcal***, you'll love reading the adventures of Darcy and Mozart in the Emerald Isle.

Click here to continue reading.

An Irish castle, a gourmet food critic, and a dead body...

Darcy Finnegan and **her trusty Schnoodle Mozart**, along with bestie Lizzie are off for a weekend soiree at Blackrock Castle.

How lucky can a girl get to cover a Michelin-starred chef in her foodie magazine?

But what she discovers is a motive driven cast of characters with a lust for murder.

Eagle-eyed Darcy notices a bottle tipped over the castle floor beside a lifeless body.

She's compelled to hunt down the mystery to the deceased victim.

Meanwhile, Mozart sniffs for clues and Lizzie sets eyes on Darcy's former flame detective Marcus Evans.

As the grand clock chimes the hour, multiple guests appear agitated and anxious.

It's a chilling scene, as guests are rattled by the thought of a killer amongst them.

Can Darcy crack the mystery before the curtain falls upon another guest?

Find out in this fast-paced whodunit mystery in Murder at Blackrock Castle.

☆☆☆☆☆ " A Delightful Irish Experience" -Amazon Reader

Read Now!

A TASTE OF MEXICO

Mole Poblano de Guajolote (Turkey in Chocolate Chile Sauce)

Servings: 4–6
Prep Time: 1 hour
Cook Time: 2–3 hours
Total Time: ~4 hours
Difficulty: Moderate

History in Every Bite

In Oaxaca, *mole negro* is arguably the most sacred of the seven famous moles, traditionally reserved for significant celebrations. It's complex and smoky, made from dried chiles, nuts, seeds, spices, and Mexican chocolate. When paired with *guajolote*—the native turkey that predates European chickens—it becomes a dish of ancestral memory. Indigenous, layered, and profound.

This version honors Oaxacan tradition and is adapted for both flavor and feasibility, while keeping it as authentic as a kitchen outside Oaxaca can manage.

Ingredients

For the Turkey:

- 4–6 slices of raw turkey or chicken
- 2–3 cups (475–710 ml) turkey or chicken broth

For the Mole Sauce:

- 4 dried pasilla chiles (or substitute ancho), stems and seeds removed
- 4 dried red New Mexico chiles (e.g., Sandia or Chimayo), stems and seeds removed
- 1–2 canned chipotle chiles in adobo
- 1 medium onion, chopped
- 2 cloves garlic, minced
- 2 medium tomatoes, peeled and chopped
- 2 tablespoons sesame seeds
- ½ cup (70 g) toasted almonds, chopped
- ½ corn tortilla, torn into pieces
- ¼ cup (40 g) raisins
- ¼ teaspoon ground cloves
- 1–2 tablespoons lard or vegetable oil

- 1 ounce (28 g) Mexican chocolate (or more to taste)

Instructions

1. Prepare the Turkey:

- In a large pot, place the turkey slices and cover with water. Add a pinch of salt and bring to a boil. Reduce heat and simmer until the turkey is cooked through and tender. Remove the turkey and set aside. Reserve 2–3 cups of the cooking broth.

2. Prepare the Chiles:

- In a dry skillet over medium heat, toast the dried chiles until they puff up and become fragrant, about 1–2 minutes per side. Be careful not to burn them.

- Place the toasted chiles in a bowl and cover with hot water. Let them soak for 20–30 minutes until softened. Drain and set aside.

3. Prepare the Mole Base:

- In the same skillet, heat 1 tablespoon of lard or vegetable oil over medium heat.

- Sauté the chopped onion and minced garlic until translucent.

- Add the peeled and chopped tomatoes, and cook until the mixture thickens.

- In a blender or food processor, combine the softened chiles, sautéed onion-garlic-tomato mixture, sesame seeds, chopped almonds, torn tortilla, raisins, ground cloves, and chipotle chiles.

- Add 1 cup of the reserved turkey broth and blend until smooth.

4. Cook the Mole Sauce:

- In a large saucepan, heat the remaining lard or oil over medium heat.

- Pour in the blended mole sauce and cook, stirring frequently, for about 10 minutes.

- Add the Mexican chocolate and stir until melted and well incorporated.

- Gradually add more reserved turkey broth to achieve a smooth, slightly thick consistency.

- Reduce heat to low and simmer the mole sauce for 30–45 minutes, stirring occasionally.

5. Combine and Serve:

- Add the cooked turkey slices to the mole sauce, ensuring they are well coated.

- Simmer for an additional 10–15 minutes to allow the flavors to meld.

- Serve the *Mole Poblano de Guajolote* hot, garnished with additional sesame seeds if desired.

Serving Suggestions

Traditionally, *Mole Poblano de Guajolote* is served with:

- *Arroz Rojo* (Mexican red rice)
- Warm corn tortillas
- Refried beans
- A sprinkle of toasted sesame seeds on top for garnish

Made in the USA
Columbia, SC
13 July 2025

60714702R00122